SEVEN WHOLE DAYS

A Health and Healing Worship Book

by

Best wishes

Howard Booth

Howard Booth

Arthur James

BOOK PUBLISHERS

© Howard Booth

World rights reserved worldwide by the publishers

Arthur James Limited
One Cranbourne Road
London N10 2BT
Great Britain

First published 1992

British Library Cataloguing-in-Publication Data

Booth, Howard
Seven Whole Days: A Health and Healing Worship Book
I. Title
264
ISBN 0-85305-325-1

Cover Design by
The Creative House, Saffron Walden, Essex

Typeset by
Stumptype, London N20 0QG

Printed and bound by
The Guernsey Press Co. Ltd, Guernsey, C.I.

SEVEN WHOLE DAYS

A Health and Healing Worship Book

by

Howard Booth

DEDICATION

This book is dedicated to the memory of
THE REVD. DR. JOHN YOUNG

Physician, Priest, Psychiatrist and Director of The
Churches' Council for Health and Healing

I first met John Young when he came to be interviewed for the post of Director of the Churches' Council for Health and Healing. He was by far the outstanding applicant for this post, combining, as he did, the skills of psychiatric medicine with the training he had received when preparing to be ordained as a non-stipendiary priest in the Church of England. After he took early retirement from his consultant's post in the National Health Service, he proceeded to Queen's College, Birmingham, as Research Fellow, looking into the Ministry of Healing and the contribution of Paul Tournier to this.

Although his time as Director of The Churches' Council for Health and Healing was comparatively short, he made a deep impression on all who knew him. He was anxious to extend the range of the Council's activities and was particularly concerned to carry on the visionary work of the founder, the late Archbishop William Temple, in developing relationships between the Church and Medicine and thus between doctors and clergy. He travelled widely, including a visit to India in the company of the former Archbishop of Canterbury, Dr. Coggan.

I shared in several conferences with him. Sheila, his wife, came along and played her part in imaginative sessions on the art of listening. They were a team in every sense of the word.

This is now being demonstrated even after his death. John established a branch office in Stafford combining the work of the Acorn Christian Healing Trust and that of CCHH. After his death financial stringency made its continuation difficult but Sheila, with the help of a number of others, established the John Young Foundation to carry on the work so effectively begun. I greatly appreciate her willingness to allow me to dedicate this Health and Healing Worship Book to his memory.

Howard Booth

CONTENTS

Introduction and Acknowledgement

Section 1

Seven Liturgies and Orders of Service   Page

No. 1 A Festival Service of Praise for Health and Healing   7

No. 2 The Oil of Healing: a Service based on Luke 10   17

No. 3 The Church is Healing   26

No. 4 An Order of Service for a Healing Communion   31

No. 5 A Healing Experience   37

No. 6 Waiting for the Rainbow   40

No. 7 The Incurable Wound   47

Section 2

Seven Sets of Additional Prayers

No. 1 Prayers of Confession and Intercession   59

No. 2 A Prayer for Wholeness   63

No. 3 Lighten our Darkness   65

No. 4 Prayers for Healing and Reconciliation   68

No. 5 Praying about Stress   73

No. 6 Praying which makes a Difference   78

No. 7 Praying with our Bodies   82

CONTENTS (continued)

Section 3

Seven Hymns   Page

No. 1   Beyond Measure   91

No. 2   A Hymn for Healing Services   92

No. 3   A Hymn for Counsellors   93

No. 4   The Wounded Healer   94

No. 5   Shalom   95

No. 6   Prayer for Healing   96

No. 7   Christ's Call   97

Section 4

Seven Meditations based on Seven Psalms

Introduction   101

No. 1   The Two Ways   Psalm   1   103

No. 2   Night Prayer   Psalm   4   106

No. 3   He Leadeth Me   Psalm   23   110

No. 4   Dealing with Moods   Psalm   42   113

No. 5   Sorry, Lord   Psalm   51   117

No. 6   Dynamic Worship   Psalm   84   120

No. 7   Wonder, Love and Praise Psalm 139   123
                                (verses 1-18 and 23-24)

Section 5

Seven General Meditations

No. 1 Singing the Creator's Song   129

No. 2 The Healing Power of Forgiveness   133

No. 3 A Journey through Life   138

No. 4 The Space Between   140

No. 5 Complementary Gospel Values   142

No. 6 Living is Loving   145

No. 7 Wholeness is God's Gift   147

Section 6

Seven Suggestions for Health and Healing Services

No. 1 A Healing Service based on the
       Meditation on Love (page 145)   154

No. 2 A Healing Service based on the
       Old Testament word 'Shalom'   157

No. 3 A Service on Preventive Health Care   160

No. 4 A Service of Anointing   163

No. 5 A Health and Healing Service to be held in
       connection with a Health Fair or Festival of Health 166

No. 6 In Quietness and Confidence (Relaxation,
       Meditation and Visualisation)   168

No. 7 Prescription for Health   173

CONTENTS (continued)

Section 7

Seven Sets of Quotations, Sentences, etc.   Page

No. 1   Health   180

No. 2   Healing   182

No. 3   Prayer   184

No. 4   Introductory Sentences   186

No. 5   Sentences for the Laying on of Hands   188

No. 6   Helpful Words and Works of Jesus
        from Alan Dale's *New World*   190

No. 7   Seven Significant Words or Phrases   192

Appendices

1.   Contributors   195

2.   Books   197

INTRODUCTION

Although the number of churches holding regular healing services is increasing year by year, there are also those who believe that, in a very real sense, every worship service has healing possibilities and can therefore be described as a healing service. Although I support the practice of holding regular, well-prepared healing services, I also accept the above position as well. Within every service of Christian worship, healings of many different kinds can and should take place. In my experience this is particularly true of services which include a celebration of Holy Communion.

As one who is constantly looking for suitable devotional material to include in healing services, I am always delighted to find new liturgies, hymns, prayers, poems, readings and particularly helpful meditations. In recent years, as I have gone around the whole of the United Kingdom sharing in conferences, retreats and quiet days, I have kept on the look out for such material and have also invited individual contributions. Then, as I have prepared my own material, I have tried it out in a variety of situations. That which seems to have been helpful I have retained to use in this new publication.

I am particularly drawn to use a variety of healing meditations which include times of silence and also utilise quiet music. In this respect the Taizé chants are always appropriate but there are other musical sources which I have found useful including classical guitar music. A helpful organist can often improvise to great effect and when minister or worship leader and organist prepare together a truly healing atmosphere can be created.

Sometimes the sermon or gospel exposition can be delivered in a meditative form. This gives time for the hearers to absorb what is offered, and to relate it to their own circumstances and make their own response. I tried this out first many years ago with considerable trepidation, but it seemed to work and I have repeated the practice on a number of occasions since.

1

As already indicated there are a number of contributions to this Worship Book which have been written by other people. These are distinguished by their names being attached at the end of their contributions. I am most grateful to them all. For added convenience I have attached a list of their names and addresses as an appendix. This raises the question of the copying of individual services and meditations, hymns etc. for congregational use. I have no objection to this for 'one-off' occasions, nor have most of my contributors. There are however one or two exceptions to this. Julie Hulme wishes to protect the copyright of the two poems, *Jericho Road* and *One*. Any requests to reproduce these should be addressed to Julie. There are also a few items which have already been published. Full details are given of both authors and publishers and I have obtained their permission to reproduce them. Again contact would need to be made with the original publishers for permission to use them. It is not likely to be withheld for 'one-off' occasions.

I have utilised a number of short quotations from various books and details are given following upon each quotation. In addition I have supplied a list of all the books referred to in a further appendix. I recommend all the books I have utilised and I apologise in advance for any omissions.

For reasons of expense and also copyright regulations it was decided not to include any music in this Worship Book. However my wife, who is a musician, has helped me in the selection of well-known tunes for the hymns. These are mentioned by name, rather than by referring to a particular book, as there are so many different hymn books in general use nowadays. As always, I am grateful to Alice for her constant support in everything I try to do. She has played the organ and piano for many of the services and meditations in this Worship Book.

In a book by Lindsay P. Pherigo entitled *The Great Physician* he says... "One of the simplest and yet most effective ways of raising a congregation's level of consciousness of the unity of the mind-soul-spirit-emotions-body complex is through carefully planned worship experiences that exemplify this integration''. I believe this to be true and this Worship Book has been planned to enable such 'healing experiences' to come alive.

Howard Booth

102a, Gawsworth Rd.,
Broken Cross,
Macclesfield,
Cheshire
SK11 8UF

Note: sentences and sections in bold type are to be said by all.

Seven whole days, not one in seven,
*   I will praise Thee;*
In my heart, though not in heaven,
*   I can raise Thee.*
Small it is, in this poor sort
*   To enrol Thee:*
E'en eternity's too short
*   To extol Thee.*

(George Herbert, 1593-1632)

Section 1

SEVEN LITURGIES
AND
ORDERS OF SERVICE

A FESTIVAL SERVICE OF PRAISE FOR HEALTH AND PRAYER FOR HEALING

Introductory sentences:

> Praise is inner health made audible.
> **Lord, teach us to adore.**
>
> Glory to the Father, and to the Son,
> and to the Holy Spirit.
> **As it was in the beginning, is now, and
> shall be for ever. Amen.**

HYMN: Jesus is Lord! Creation's voice proclaims it

Opening Prayer:

> **Father, help us to worship you in spirit and in truth,
> that our consciences may be quickened by your
> holiness,
> our minds nourished by your truth,
> our imagination purified by your beauty,
> our hearts opened by your love,
> our wills surrendered to your purpose;
> and may all this be gathered up in adoration
> as we ascribe glory, praise and honour to you alone,
> through Jesus Christ our Lord. Amen.**

A TIME OF REPENTANCE

> **Lord, we have sinned and we know that our failure has
> affected our inward harmony and thereby our health
> and well-being.**

7

Leader: Jesus, remember me, when you come into your
Kingdom.

People: **Jesus, remember me, when you come into your
Kingdom.**

**Lord, we have failed miserably in some of our
relationships and this has affected other people's lives
adversely and has damaged our own lives.**

Leader: Jesus, remember me..........

People: **Jesus, remember me..........**

**Lord, we have sinned by not taking care of our friends
and neighbours; we have also taken insufficient notice
of the needs of those in other lands. Indeed we have
been so obsessed with ourselves that we have failed to
be aware of their pain and suffering.**

Leader: Jesus, remember me..........

People: **Jesus, remember me..........**

Silence (for private confession)

Leader: Be at peace. God has promised that if we confess
our sins we shall be forgiven, so, in his name I
say to you: "Your sins are forgiven".

People: **Amen: thanks be to God.**

THE MINISTRY OF THE WORD

HYMN: Open, Lord, my inward ear

A READING FROM THE OLD TESTAMENT OR THE EPISTLES

HYMN: Alleluia, alleluia, give thanks to the risen Lord

A READING FROM THE GOSPEL

SERMON

Silence for reflection

INTERCESSIONS

We pray for the Church,
for its life and witness,
and for all who work and pray
to heal the hurts of needy people.

Lord, in your mercy,
Hear our prayer.

Deliver us good Lord,
From every harmful practice and process,
From every abuse of nature,
And from every misuse of science
that facilitates disease or inhibits the
fullest health of body, mind and spirit.

Lord, in your mercy,
Hear our prayer.

Bless all who care for the sick in our local communities.
Help them to look beneath the surface and so discern the
real needs of their clients and patients.

9

Then give them the wisdom and insight which
creates sensitivity in their relationships, thus
enabling deep healing to take place.

Lord, in your mercy,
Hear our prayer.

Continue to bless the ministries of our many hospices and
the supportive work of the Macmillan and Madam Curie
Nurses.
Grant adequate, inward resources to all who care for the
dying. Help them, through their own inward peace and
serenity to generate faith, hope and trust. Give them the
assurance that love triumphs in the end.

Lord, in your mercy,
Hear our prayer.

(Individual intercessions are now invited)

Leader: And now to God the Father, God the Son and God the
Holy Spirit be ascribed glory, honour and praise now and for
ever. Amen.

THE MINISTRY OF THE LAYING ON OF HANDS

Hymn: O Christ the healer, we have come...

*(The people are invited to come forward to the communion rail or
any other appointed place. They may come for healing of many
kinds: wrong relationships, jealousies, false ambitions, physical
needs or for the gift of inward peace. Those who remain in their
places are invited to concentrate in prayer for those who are coming
to receive ministry)*

(During this time prayer choruses may be sung such as:)

> Be still and know that I am God.

> In you, O Lord, I put my trust.

> I am the Lord who healeth thee.

> Shalom, my friend, God's peace, my friend,
> Be with you now.
> And stay with you in all you do,
> Shalom, Shalom.

> Healing hands of Jesus Christ,
> Now be laid on me.
> Healing hands of Jesus Christ,
> Now be laid on me.
> Touch me, stir me,
> Unfold me, love me,
> Healing hands of Jesus Christ,
> Now be laid on me.

> These my hands you gave to me,
> I give back to you.
> These my hands you gave to me,
> I give back to you.
> Take them, guide them,
> Bless them, use them.
> These my hands you gave to me,
> I give back to you.

THE LORD'S SUPPER

(The celebrant invites us to share with one another a sign of peace)

HYMN: Lord Jesus Christ, you have come to us

THE GREAT PRAYER OF THANKSGIVING

The Lord be with you.
And also with you.

Lift up your hearts.
We lift them up to the Lord.

Let us give thanks to the Lord our God.
It is right to give him thanks and praise.

It is indeed right —
It is our duty and our joy,
to give you thanks, Holy Father,
through Jesus Christ our Lord.

Through him you have created us in your image;
through him you have freed us from sin and death;
through him you have made us your own people
by the gift of the Holy Spirit.

Therefore with angels and archangels and all the company
of heaven we proclaim your great and glorious name, for
ever praising you and saying:

Holy, Holy, Holy, Lord of power and might,
Heaven and earth are full of your glory. All glory to
your name.
Blessed is he who comes in the name of the Lord.
Hosanna in the highest.

Hear us, Father,
through Christ your Son our Lord,
and grant that by the power of the Holy Spirit
these gifts of bread and wine
may be to us his body and his blood.

Who in the same night that he was betrayed,
took bread and gave you thanks;
he broke it and gave it to his disciples, saying,
"Take, eat; this is my body which is given for you;
do this in remembrance of me".
In the same way, after supper, he took the cup
and gave you thanks;
he gave it to them saying:
"Drink this all of you;
this is my blood of the new covenant
which is shed for you and for many
for the forgiveness of sins.
Do this as often as you drink it,
in remembrance of me".

Dying you destroyed our death,
Rising, you restored our life.
Lord Jesus, come in glory.

Therefore, Father,
proclaiming his saving death and resurrection
and looking for his coming in glory,
we celebrate with this bread and this cup
his one perfect sacrifice.

Accept through him, our great high priest,
this our sacrifice of thanks and praise,
and grant that we who eat this bread and drink this cup

13

may be renewed by your Spirit
and grow into his likeness.

**Through Jesus Christ our Lord,
by whom, and with whom and in whom,
all honour and glory be yours, Father,
now and for ever. Amen.**

(The celebrant breaks the bread in the sight of the people)

The gifts of God for the people of God.
**Jesus Christ is holy,
Jesus Christ is Lord,
to the glory of God the Father.**

THE SHARING OF THE BREAD AND WINE

(The Celebrant and Assistants receive the bread and wine)

INVITATION TO COMMUNION

Jesus is the Lamb of God,
who takes away the sins of the world.
Happy are those who are called to his supper.
**Lord, I am not worthy to receive you,
But only say the word, and I shall be healed.**

THE COMMUNION OF THE PEOPLE

(During the communion the following choruses may be sung:)

Father, we adore you,
Lay our lives before you:
How we love you.

Jesus, we adore you...

Spirit, we adore you...

Turn your eyes upon Jesus,
Look full in his wonderful face,
And the things of earth will grow strangely dim,
In the light of his glory and grace.

POST-COMMUNION PRAYER:

**Almighty God,
we thank you for feeding us
with the body and blood of your Son, Jesus Christ.
Through him we offer you our souls and bodies
to be a living sacrifice.
Send us out
in the power of your Spirit,
to live and work
to your praise and glory. Amen.**

HYMN: Thou whose Almighty Word

THE BLESSING

**The peace of God which passes all understanding,
keep our hearts and minds in the knowledge and love
of God and of his Son, Jesus Christ our Lord; and the
blessing of God almighty, the Father, the Son and the
Holy Spirit remain with us always. Amen.**

*(After the blessing we make a great ring around the Church joining
hands and singing:)*

"Bind us together, Lord"

(We then leave the Church singing joyfully:)

"You shall go out with joy and be led forth with peace"

NOTES AND ACKNOWLEDGEMENTS:

1. This Service was first used at the Methodist School of Fellowship Conference held at Swanwick in August 1991. It was prepared by Howard Booth with the help of Norman and Margaret Wallwork.

2. The first introductory sentence is taken from the writings of C.S. Lewis.

3. The opening prayer is an adaptation of a quotation by William Temple and is by Bishop Morris Maddocks.

4. The suggested hymns and choruses can be found in a variety of hymn and song books including *Hymns and Psalms, Mission Praise* and *Power Praise*.

5. The responses in *A Time of Repentance* can be sung to settings by the Taizé Community.

6. The choruses *Healing hands of Jesus Christ* and *These my hands you gave to me* are by the author and are sung to the tune set for *Spirit of the Living God*.

THE OIL OF HEALING

A Service based on Luke 10:25-37

INVOCATION
   (Pause for silence)

   Let us remember that we are in the presence of God,
   who knows us and knows our needs,
   and who loves us with a love that is both gentle and
   strong, unchanging and eternal.

   (Pause)

   O living God,
   you are reaching out to us in love,
   so draw us near to yourself here, now,
   that we may know your presence
   and find joy in the peace that you have given us.
   For Christ's sake we ask it, Amen.

HYMN *(of praise and adoration)*

ADORATION AND CONFESSION

   O Living God, we praise you,
   Live in us now.

   O Living God,
   you are Father and Mother to us in our beginning,
   creating, protecting and nurturing us throughout our
   pilgrimage, and day by day we are nourished by your love.

We confess that we have not always lived in trust,
and ask that we may learn afresh the ways of holy
dependence,
knowing ourselves to be sustained by your care,
and upheld by your joy.
O Living God, we praise you,
Live in us now.

O Living Jesus,
you are our companion and friend along the way,
partnering us in peace and in peril, in promise and in
pain,
and day by day we are kept in your truth and your life.
We confess that we have often evaded the cross,
and ask that we may learn afresh the ways of faithful
obedience,
that we may die with you, and rise again with you
to eternal glory.
O Living God, we praise you,
Live in us now.

O Living Spirit,
you are breath and life to us, light and fire,
enabling and lifting us when we fall,
and we are strengthened through your grace and power.
We confess that so often we have tried to live only with
our own strength,
and ask that we may learn afresh how to acknowledge our
weakness,
for it is when we are broken that your power
is made complete in us.
O living God, we praise you,
Live in us now.

PSALM

> O Lord, do not be angry:
> I cannot bear your wrath, when I need your mercy,
> Be gracious, I am so desolate.
>
> There is so much pain within me;
> I am torn inside and I ache in my soul
> while I wait for your mercy.
>
> Turn towards me as my Deliverer,
> and as my Saviour, come to me in your everlasting love.
> For if I die, can I still praise you?
> How can I glorify you in the depths?
>
> I am so worn, so tired, so dreary;
> Tears are always close at hand,
> I am so weighed down,
> and no one seems to be on my side.
>
> And yet you have heard my prayer,
> You will answer me,
> So begone all my adversaries,
> there is no victory for you here.

> *(Adapted from Psalm 6)*

HYMN

READING: Luke 10: 25-37

REFLECTING ON THE GOSPEL

JERICHO ROAD

It was here they found me,
already deep within the vale of death,
the path thin and walls of blunt rock
steep on every side,
Cool here, shadowed respite from the noon's heat,
hammer-hard,
yet I felt the threatening of shade
just before they stabbed out of the dark.

Here they left me,
spread out in the belly of the rock,
my blood receding into sand
and all the world a firelit whirl of pain.

Twice I heard the footsteps,
tried to stir, to beg for mercy, shout my name
into the void.
Some groaning made them pause,
consider,
then move on.
I, listening to the fading presence,
beckoned death, oblivion.

So it was here he found me,
Firm hands, warm words,
soothing moisture, cool,
The sting of wine to cleanse the wounds,
and oil to ease,
linen pads to rest, protect,
and then the strength of arm and shoulder
lifting, setting me across his patient beast.

I looked then: something about his clothes,
his accent said,
Samaritan!

I had not looked for mercy from his kind.
I had not thought to find such love in one
ignored, despised and hated.
And I had not expected that his hands,
so scarred,
could be so gentle, nor his face,
so tired,
could be so strong,
until I saw his eyes.

FOR THOUGHT AND DISCUSSION

1. Where do we look for the healing of our wounds:
    physical, emotional, spiritual, the healing of the memory?

2. Do we miss what the healing Christ offers us because we
    are not prepared to receive it in unexpected ways?

RESPONSE TO THE GOSPEL

O Living God, come as the One who created and sustains
us, who walks the road with us, even in difficult and
dangerous places.
**O God of mercy, come to us in our brokenness, remain
with us even when we believe ourselves to be utterly
forsaken.**
O Wounded Christ, come to us as the One who has borne
our pain and sorrow on the cross.

**O Christ the healer, crucified and risen, come to us
with the scars on your hands and feet, the hole in your
side.**
O Spirit of Consolation, come to us as a balm and a
comfort,
as the oil of cleansing and encouragement.
**O strength of the Living God, come to us, bear us up,
and bring us to the house of healing.**
God of our life: Maker, Redeemer, Friend, may we wait
for you in courage and in trust,
**That in our pain you may bring comfort, and in our
sorrow, peace: this day and forever.**

HYMN

INTERCESSORY PRAYERS

Let us bring before God our own need for healing, and
our burden for God's world:

We remember before God the pain and trouble of all who
are broken in body, mind and spirit.....

(Pause)

God of Love: **We trust in your mercy,**
We remember before God all whose pilgrimage takes
them through difficult and dangerous places.....

(Pause)

God of Love: **We trust in your mercy.**
We remember before God all who feel abandoned and
alone, their pain and their cries for help ignored.....

(Pause)

God of Love: **We trust in your mercy.**
We remember before God all who are challenged to
respond to the needs of others.....

(Pause)

God of Love: **We trust in your mercy.**

God of Love and Mercy, you know our needs,
You feel the pain with our pain,
You hear our prayers of word and heart,
You respond to the truth and the love that you have given
us,
And so in gratitude and trust, we leave our concerns with
you, offering all into your hands as we pray together.....

(The Lord's Prayer)

OFFERTORY

COMMUNION HYMN *(if appropriate)*

THANKSGIVING

Creator God, in the beginning you were there bringing
new life into being, and despite the wounds of sin and
pain that we have brought upon ourselves and your
world, you are still with us, sustaining us, guiding us,
protecting us.

Creator God, we give you thanks and praise.

Loving God, you have never abandoned us, and at the
time of your choosing you sent among us your son, our
Lord and Saviour, Jesus Christ, who lived in our midst

as a healer, teacher and friend, who forgave sins with
your authority and delivered ordinary people from the
evil that had overpowered them.

Loving God, we give you thanks and praise.

Holy God, in your Son you have called us to yourself, to
live as he lived, and to follow him in the way of death
and resurrection. For though he had done no wrong he
was cruelly and unjustly slain, suffering great torment of
body, mind and spirit. Though he had committed no sin,
he was denounced, mocked and betrayed to his death, by
many of those who had praised him, and in his
desolation he felt abandoned by God. Yet on the third
day you raised him from the dead, showing that your
love is stronger than any evil or wickedness, even the
power of death itself.

Holy God, we give you thanks and praise.

And so it was that our Lord Jesus Christ, on the night in
which he was betrayed..... (Here follow the Words of
Institution).

Comforting God, you are our enabler, our advocate and
our friend,
move among us in our communion,
accept our worship and our praise,
and strengthen us in the desire to serve you.
Grant us the gifts and fruits of your life within us,
increase in us the dedication of our offering,
and hold us in your love,
that we may come with you to the home of glory. Amen.

THE BREAKING OF THE BREAD AND THE SHARING OF THE BREAD AND WINE

(Those who wish to receive the laying on of hands remain at the communion rail or otherwise indicate)

HYMN

BENEDICTION

> May God who takes with you the pilgrim way,
> lead you in trust and peace all your days,
> that, whether on the plains of joy or in the vale of shadow,
> you may know the touch of tenderness
> and grace which makes us whole. Amen.

THE GRACE

Julie M. Hulme

THE CHURCH IS HEALING

Suggestions for a Worship Service to enable a local Church to get a clearer vision of the healing ministry.

> The Church is called to be a community in which the total healing work of the Holy Spirit is taught, sought and experienced. The Spirit of Healing is present in the worship, sacraments, preaching, prayer, fellowship, pastoral and social ministry... This is its *normal* activity and *all* its members are called to be involved in it.
>
> *Methodist Conference Statement 1977.*

In these days a great deal is being said and written about the churches' healing ministry. Some see it as a specialised form of ministry requiring a great deal of preparation and training. While proper preparation and training are a feature of every aspect of Christian ministry, the above statement makes it clear that we are considering the healing ministry as being a proper part of the life of every church. It is not something extra to be grafted on but something which is an essential part of the whole. This service will proceed through four stages and each will present ideas for thought and reflection; these will then be offered to God in prayer.

HYMN

PRAYER

God, our Father, you sent your only Son, Jesus, on earth to heal a broken-hearted and wounded world. He had compassion on those who called on him for help and healing. People asked for health of body and he released them from their sins as well.

He touched the sick and guilt-laden, and they walked away in health and freedom of spirit. Visit us now with your saving power that we too may be released in body, mind and spirit to praise your healing grace.   Amen.

1. RECOGNISE WHAT IS ALREADY HAPPENING

You do not have to start a healing ministry in a local Church; you have to realise that it is already in existence. Wherever people are being forgiven of their sins following upon penitence and confession, there is healing. Where people are being loved, cared for and understood, there is healing. Wherever there is prayer being offered for the sick and lonely, there is healing. This is where we begin. Other developments may follow but let us now affirm the value of what is already happening.

> *(Quiet Taizé music could now be played while the congregation gives thanks for their church's existing healing ministry. Various aspects of the church's life can be affirmed both by the minister/ leader and members of the congregation)*

2. CREATE THE RIGHT ATMOSPHERE FOR HONEST SHARING

We wear masks and try to hide both our needs and our spiritual poverty. We tend to live make-believe Christian lives which put on a show, but lack authenticity. Sharing our hurts, our puzzled minds, our unanswered questions, brings release and consequently greater reality. But how do we create the right atmosphere for this honest sharing? Perhaps it all begins at the centre when those in positions of leadership and

27

responsibility, set the pace. But it must never be artificial or contrived. Real sharing brings healing release.

(As more quiet music is played there may be those who are willing to share their own sense of need and then the minister/leader can gather it all up in prayer)

PRAYER

3. DEVELOP THE ART OF LISTENING

It is easy to think that we are good listeners when, in fact, we are not. The art of listening can be taught although some types of personality find it difficult. Anne Long's book *Listening* provides abundant material for training groups. Relationships have to be built; there has to be an exploration of the realities which the person wants to share; then understanding may follow and this stimulates action. There must always be encouragement.

(Quiet music again with some positive statements about listening being emphasised)

4. PLAN TO ENABLE HEALING EXPERIENCES

Healing experiences are of many different kinds. Those who have always felt insecure because of inadequate childhood experiences, can be helped by feeling loved and affirmed. Dark experiences can leave unhealthy memories and these can be released through good counselling aided by sacramental confession. After due preparation needy people can receive direct ministry through prayer and the laying on of hands. The basis is a really loving and caring Church community which is not sentimental in its approach but realistic and absolutely honest. There must be expectant faith but all our expectations must leave the ultimate outcome in God's hands. Healing experiences come via different pathways and often a combination of several different approaches: medical, psychological, spiritual and simple channels like tender, loving care.

(More quiet music with various possibilities
for continuing healing experiences being outlined
and God's help and guidance sought)

A PRAYER FOR INDIVIDUALS

God our Father, I turn to you in my unrest because I cannot see the way out of the present situation which troubles my spirit. In confusion I turn to you for help and guidance because you alone can help me and nothing is impossible for you. Light up my life with faith, strengthen me in hope and fill me with love, so that I may rest in your providence, which alone knows what is for my peace.   **Amen.**

HYMN

BLESSING

Notes:

1.   Anne Long's book *Listening* is published by Daybreak Books, a series from Darton, Longman and Todd.

2.   My own book *Healing through Caring* contains a series of six simple studies for use in groups. It contains material which could be used in the above service and in house groups with a purpose. It is published by Arthur James Ltd.

AN ORDER OF SERVICE FOR A HEALING COMMUNION

Greeting

HYMN OF ADORATION

(A candle is lit as words from the Bible about light and healing are spoken)

A TIME OF QUIET REFLECTION

CONFESSION:

Mighty God, loving Saviour, you know all about us; we can never hide from you, we are never lost to you; you know our weakness; you know our sickness.

Mighty God, loving Saviour;
We come to you for healing.

We need your forgiving grace;
We need the wholeness only you can give;
Create in us a clean heart, O God,
And renew a right spirit within us.

Mighty God, loving Saviour;
We come to you for healing.

We have so misused our own lives;
We have so abused and wounded the life of your earth;
We have so feebly shared in your overflowing love;
We need your healing for all creation;

31

We need your spirit of compassion and peace.

Mighty God, loving Saviour,
We come to you for healing;
Forgive us and restore us to true life.

The word of Jesus to us is sure: I have come that you might
have life, Life in all its fulness. Your sins are forgiven.
Your faith makes you whole.

THE PEACE IS SHARED

HYMN *(with a healing theme)*

BIBLE READING(S)

SERMON OR MEDITATION

INTERCESSIONS (For those in need of healing; for those
engaged in various kinds of healing work, and for healing
within the body of human society and in earth's body.)

HYMN *(relating to Communion. The offering may be taken here
if desired)*

THANKSGIVING AT THE HOLY TABLE *(Stand if
appropriate)*

Lift up your hearts;
We lift them to the Lord.

Let us give thanks to the Lord our God;
It is right to give him thanks and praise.

Mighty God, Saviour of the world,
We lift our hearts to you
Thankful for all you have given us through Jesus:
the gift of life, the forgiveness of sins, the hope of health,
the promise of your Kingdom,
Confidence in your love for every one of your children.

For, at the last meal that Jesus shared with his disciples
before his death,
He took bread in his hands of compassion,
Gave thanks to you and broke the bread,
Saying, "Take this bread, all of you, and eat it,
This is my body given for you,
Do this to remember me".

Saviour of all, with this bread
We celebrate your healing love.

Then Jesus took the cup, offered thanks, and gave the cup to
his disciples, saying,
"Take this all of you and drink from it,
This is the cup of the new covenant
sealed in my blood, shed for you and for many,
for the forgiveness of sins,
Do this to remember me".

Saviour of all, with this cup,
We celebrate the new life of your Kingdom.

(All may sit for a brief time of quiet)

As this bread was once scattered seed,
O, Bread of Life,
Sown in the earth to die
and rise to new life,

So gather all your children together
in the one body that is your purpose for us.
Restore the broken life of your creation,
Heal the disfigured body of your world,
Draw us all into yourself, into new life,
into wholeness through your cross
and in the power of your risen life.

THE BREAKING

When we break bread together,
do we not share in the body of Christ?

**We who are many are one body,
for we all share the one bread.**

We will lift up the cup of salvation

**And call on the name of the Lord,
who forgives all our sin
and heals all our sickness.**

THE SHARING OF BREAD AND WINE *(if possible with the people in a circle)*

THE LAYING ON OF HANDS

THE FINAL THANKSGIVING

Having shared in the feast that is God's sign of his coming
Kingdom, we pray in confidence and hope,

Come, Lord Jesus, come to make all things new.
Even as you have touched us with new life,
And filled us with strong hope,
Unite all things in your fulness,
That all creation may rejoice in your goodness.
For the Kingdom, the Power and the Glory
Are yours alone for ever and ever.   Amen.

HYMN OF THANKSGIVING OR COMMITMENT TO SHARE GOD'S HEALING WORK IN THE WORLD

THE BLESSING AND COMMISSION

The God of peace will be with you to bless you
and to grant you his peace at all times,
Peace beyond our understanding,
that purifies heart, mind and body,
until his Kingdom comes.   **Amen.**

Having shared this feast of God's love,
Go into the world to share God's love through your life.
In the name of Christ.   **Amen.**

The following verses may then be sung...

Peace is flowing like a river,
Flowing out through you and me,
Spreading out into the desert,
Setting all the captives free.

Hope is flowing...

Love is flowing...

(This service was devised by the Revd. Dr. E.J. Lott and has appeared in the magazine *Health and Healing* published by the Division of Social Responsibility of the Methodist Church)

A HEALING EXPERIENCE

PRAISING — LISTENING — RESPONDING

A brief Act of Worship suitable for use at the close of a Day Conference

Introduction

PRAISING

HYMN   We give Immortal Praise. *or*
              Praise to the Lord, the Almighty.

Remain standing and join in...
THE KOREAN CREED:

We believe in one God, maker and ruler of all things, Father of us all and source of all goodness, beauty and truth and love. We believe in Jesus Christ, God manifest in the flesh, our Teacher, Example and Redeemer, the Saviour of the world. We believe in the Holy Spirit, God present with us for guidance, for comfort and for strength. We believe in the forgiveness of sins, the life of love and prayer, and of grace equal to every need. We believe in the Word of God contained in the Old and New Testaments as the sufficient rule of faith and practice. We believe in the Church as the fellowship for worship and for service of all united to our Living Lord. We believe in the Kingdom of God as the divine rule in human society and in the fellowship of all people under the Fatherhood of God. We believe in the final triumph of righteousness and in the life everlasting.

SING OR SAY THE TE DEUM OR PSALM 8

PRAYER AND THE LORD'S PRAYER

HYMN: Give me joy in my heart, keep me praising

LISTENING

BIBLE READING: Mark 1:35-45 *or* other appropriate passage.

EXPOSITION — Part 1

(A time of quiet)

EXPOSITION — Part 2

(A time of quiet)

RESPONDING

> Jesus, open our eyes,
> Let us see your glory;
> Help us to love our neighbours —
> And listen to their story.
>
> Jesus, guide our hands,
> Let them feel your glory,
> Help us to touch our neighbour's needs —
> By telling them your story.
>
> Jesus, fill our minds,
> Let them think your glory;
> Then help them to communicate —
> The wonders of your story.

Jesus, guide our feet,
All the way to glory;
As we walk may others feel —
The impact of your story.

Jesus, be our friend,
Fill us with your glory;
Help us to experience —
The meaning of your story.

(Those present are invited to join hands and spend a few moments in quietness each seeking to be a channel of God's healing grace to all others present)

HYMN: "Bind us together, Lord"

THE PEACE

THE GRACE

WAITING FOR THE RAINBOW

A Service for Healing based on the story of Noah, and on Matthew 7:7-11.

(This Service is designed for use with a small group or congregation, whose members should be seated in a semi-circle or full circle, with a small table in the middle where all can see it. Place a cross on the table, with a lighted candle before it to symbolise the living presence of Christ. Each person present will need a Bible, pencil and two pieces of paper. You will also need a plain bowl or basket and a second bowl decorated with paper or material in rainbow colours.)

ENTERING INTO PRAYER

As people join the group they are given a pencil and paper. When all are gathered the Leader welcomes them and invites them to spend a few moments writing down responses to the following questions:

1. How do you feel? (The response to this might be a list of words to describe how they are feeling such as rushed, hot and bothered, calm, expectant etc.)

2. What concerns are you carrying with you today? (An opportunity to note down any worries, burdens, anxieties that they have or any other 'baggage' that they feel they have brought with them.)

3. Have you come to pray for a particular need for healing? (Such needs may be for healing of body, mind, spirit, memory, relationships, or a combination of these in an individual or a community.)

When the responses are complete the Leader suggests that
papers are folded and held in lap or hand during the first part
of the praying...

(Allow the group to settle into silence)

The Leader reads Matthew 7:7-8.

(Pause)

God of our everyday, you love us.
You know us as we really are.
You know our needs before we ask.
And you are always there for us,
available, ready, eager to receive us, cherish us,
lavish us with your gifts.

Yet sometimes we find it hard to be honest before you.
It is not easy to humble ourselves,
to allow our wills to be broken, crushed,
so that we can be reborn,
or melted down, so that love can make us anew.
But we desire to love you,
and so we offer ourselves to you again,
unfolding our hearts to you,
bringing ourselves forward as we really are,
so that you may be free to deal with our troubles and
difficulties, our humours and our moods,
and we can be truly open to the deeper, cleansing and healing
work of your Spirit in our lives, and in the lives of those for
whom we pray.

THE LORD'S PRAYER

(In the silence after the prayer, the plain basket or bowl is passed around and the papers are collected. The basket is placed on the table before the lighted candle)

A RESPONSIVE MEDITATION

God who loves us asks us to come in honesty and humility, in brokenness of spirit and with crucified pride. Only so can we worship in Spirit and in Truth.

O God, we are enclosed in your caring.
O Lord, we are held in your love.

God who loves us, calls us to follow the paths of right and wholeness, peace and reconciliation. Only so can we be healed, to bring wholeness to others.

O God, we are enclosed in your caring.
O Lord, we are held in your love.

God who loves us, urges us to bring in our hearts the concerns of our households, our communities and all creation. Only so can Christ's ministry to the world be completed.

O God, we are enclosed in your caring.
O Lord, we are held in your love.

God who loves us, commands us to build places of hospitality, houses of healing within our hearts and our communities. Only so will the world see the love of Christ in us and believe.

O God, we are enclosed in your caring.
O Lord, we are held in your love.

God who loves us requires us to offer our trust and complete
dependence to himself through Jesus Christ. Only so will we be
carried as we ride the waters of death and destruction.

O God, we are enclosed in your caring.
O Lord, we are held in your love.

God who loves us has never forgotten us. Though we might feel
ourselves to be swamped and drowning, to be lost and
abandoned, we are carried in his memory. Though we may be
troubled and doubtful, anxious and afraid, we are contained in
his heart. We send out our prayers like doves, and in return we
receive the signs of hope.

O God, we are enclosed in your caring.
O Lord, we are held in your love.

READING: Genesis 9: 8-16.

O God, we are enclosed in your caring.
O Lord, we are held in your love.

READING: Matthew 7: 7-11.

O God, we are enclosed in your caring.
O Lord, we are held in your love.

REFLECTION UPON THE GOSPEL

Read Matthew 7: 7-11 through again and this time together. Then consider the following questions in small groups or in pairs:

1.   What is God's basic attitude towards us? Arising from this what does he promise to do?

2.   Do you think that the promises refer to spiritual blessings or to the whole of life?

3.   How is this good news for you and for those about whom you are concerned?

4.   God is ready to give to us, but how do we open ourselves to receive?

RESPONSE TO THE WORD

(The Leader invites those present to use their second piece of paper to write down the name of a person or situation for whom they wish to pray. Or they may write their own name or a simple phrase to indicate their intention. These prayer requests may be the same as the concerns they noted down earlier, but this does not matter, nor does it matter if they wish to leave their paper blank. A blank sheets says that we are waiting upon God, not that we are indifferent. The pieces of paper are then folded and placed in the second rainbow tray or bowl.)

O God in your love for us
Open our hearts to receive you.

Loving God, you have given us your promise, you have written your covenant within our hearts, you have assured our blessing. May we so turn to you, that all our life becomes harmonised with your will for us. May we see signs of your presence, be sustained within your creative power, and live within your remembrance.

O God in your love for us
Open our hearts to receive you.

Loving God, you have told us to ask for good things at your hand. You have told us to seek you. You have told us to knock at the door of heaven. And so we come to ask for ourselves and for others. We seek you with our whole heart and we knock in confidence and trust.

O God in your love for us
Open our hearts to receive you.

A TIME OF SILENCE (Here there is an opportunity for people to pray in pairs for those needs which particularly concern them or simply to wait on God alone. The leader could offer to pray with any who indicate their desire and this could be accompanied by the laying on of hands.)

PRAYER OF DEDICATION/BENEDICTION

Creator God, you brought the world from chaos in the beginning, and you are constantly active in renewal and re-creation; sustain us and provide for us, nourish and enliven us, that we may be remade in your image —

Living God, uphold us
That our joy may be complete.

Lord Jesus Christ, you carried our burdens on the Cross,
and you still embrace a world of sorrow with your love,
accompany us on our journey,
that we may be faithful in our pilgrimage —

Living God, uphold us
That our joy may be complete.

Holy Spirit, you are our comforter, advocate and friend,
and you are active in our midst to build us in love and faith
and hope,
stir us in our weakness and frailty,
that we may be alight with your love, and alive with your
peace.

Living God, uphold us
That our joy may be complete.

Living God, Creator, Redeemer and Friend, we offer ourselves
again as a people baptised into your sacred way of truth: a way
that leads us through suffering and death to a life that is now
and for ever. Take us onward on our way, held within your
promises, and grant us courage as we wait, with those we love,
for the fulfilment of your reign amongst us.

And now may God the Father, who made the rainbow a sign of
his mercy, God the Son, who fashioned his body into a Cross
for our sakes, and God the Spirit, who searches the depths of
life, guard, guide and keep us all, this day and forever. Amen.

Julie M. Hulme

THE INCURABLE WOUND

Praying for the pain of the world

*(This service of intercession for the world is based upon the
experience of Jeremiah and the testimony of John the Baptist, that
Jesus is the Lamb of God who takes away the sin of the world. To
help in the reflection on the gospel, you may like to collect a
number of photographs from newspapers and magazines of crowd
scenes, or unknown, anonymous figures either from Britain or
overseas. For the extempore prayers of intercession you will need a
map of the world, drawing pins or some other means of marking the
map, a supply of candles or nightlights, and matches.)*

INVOCATION

O Holy God, sovereign in grace and mercy,
call us to yourself,
that we may come in penitence and trust.
Draw us into the circle of blessing,
that we may live in praise.
Remind us in our worship and in our living,
that you are love and mercy,
love and peace,
love and joy,
this day and forever. Amen.

HYMN

PRAYERS OF ADORATION AND CONFESSION

Living God, you receive us into your presence,
and we find here a place of welcome.

You bring us into your home,
and we find here a house of hospitality,
where all can come with their need.

(Pause)

O living Creator, O generous Compassion,
you are our place of refuge.
Here we can hide, here we can rest,
here we can learn to face again
our weakness and our frailty.
Here we can be nourished to face again
the fury of the world.

Living God, we seek in you the bread of life.

We do not come for ourselves alone,
but for our community, our nation, our world.
We come in penitence and trust for those around us,
to whom we are bound by ties of faith, knowledge, kinship.

(Pause)

We also come in penitence and trust for those who are not
bound to us,
those who we do not know, and perhaps do not understand;
those who are different, distant, separate, and so many.
We come in penitence because together we have failed in love.
We have failed in mercy. We have failed in justice.
We have not kept your commandments of grace.
We have not carried your cross. We have not fed your lambs.
We have not built up your kingdom.

Living God, we seek in you the mercy of renewal.

Living God, as a community, as a nation, even as your Church
we have turned away from the things which give life,
and have sought the powers of death.
We have lived as people of dust, not as children of heaven.
We recognise our failure.
We confess our wrongdoing.
We acknowledge the evils in our midst.

(Pause)

Yet in Christ, you are calling us again in trust.
Once more, to know ourselves forgiven.
Once more, to turn to our best love, our primary obedience.
Once more, to pledge our allegiance to the One who through
life and death, and life beyond death,
restores what is broken,
binds up what is perilously wounded,
and heals what is desperately diseased.

Living God, we seek in you the grace of healing.

Living God, we come to you bearing the incurable wound of
the world,
hearing, all too clearly, the unceasing cry of the world's pain.
We are part of the world, we cannot escape it,
and in our own small way, we have often added to the tale of
grief,
but you have received us, forgiven us, and now you seek to
encourage us to be part of the world's healing, agents of the
world's resurrection, seeds of a new beginning.
This task, this transformation
is utterly beyond us, and so in trust and complete dependence
we turn again to you.

Living God, we seek in You the bread of life.
Living God, we seek in You the grace of healing.
Living God, we seek in You the mercy of renewal.

READING: Jeremiah 8:18 - 9:11.

PSALM

How long, O Lord, how long
will you turn away your face,
will you leave me in oblivion?
How long, O Lord, how long
must I carry in my soul
the burden of my pain,
while my foe delights in triumph?
Consider me, my Sovereign,
and answer me, my God.
Gladden my eyes with hope,
enliven my thanksgiving,
lest my foes prevail, rejoice, exult.

For I have trusted in your love so sure,
and I sing your power to save.
I will shout in song your blessing,
your abundance, never-failing,
flowing out from your compassion,
to this lonely voice, your servant,
to this one.

(Based on Psalm 13)

HYMN

READING: John 1: 21-34.

REFLECTION ON THE GOSPEL. *(Distribute the pictures of crowds and anonymous faces. Invite those present to study their picture during the meditation.)*

ONE

You are just one in the crowd,
unnoticed and ignored;
ordinary in expression,
insignificant in dress;
a number, just one in a thousand;
a figure on paper, a name on a form —
signature scrawled unremarkably amongst many —
once seen, forever unremembered.

There is no reason why this one life
should draw attention.
There is no news in faithfulness, poverty, work,
in humour and generosity,
gentleness and grace — all these
are the stuff of anonymity,
a life lived in dull and unrelenting boredom,
unmarked by any spasm of drama,
any spark of heroism,
any demonstration, rise or fall.

You are just one one in the crowd —
a crowd that has moods, personality, potential
for lynchmob or carnival —
but you are just one face, one mind, one body,
easily glossed over or wiped out:
       one more in the queue to the counter,
       one more in the line along the trench,
       one more in the train to the gas chambers.
One less Christ in the world.

FOR REFLECTION AND DISCUSSION

1. Do you find it easy or difficult to see the face of Christ in other people?

2. What are the attitudes, beliefs and behaviour which make it more difficult to see Christ in another human being?

3. What is it that helps us to see Jesus in others? How do we open our eyes, our minds, our hearts?

4. Should there be limits? What is the cost of such openness?

RESPONSE TO THE GOSPEL

Living God, you have called us to see in each other the face of Christ.

O Lord, open our eyes that we may see.

Living God, you have commanded us to love our neighbours.

O Lord, direct our wills into the way of obedience.

Living God, you require us to love each other as you have loved us.

O Lord, break down our unlawful pride so that we may be one in spirit.

Living God, you draw us to yourself, so that we may find ourselves whole and our communities healed.

O Lord, write your new covenant upon our hearts, so that we may live it out in our everyday.

HYMN

PRAYERS OF INTERCESSION

(As each petition is made, a candle is lit, and a mark made on a map of the world. Alternatively if the service is being held in the round, small nightlights could be used and positioned on a world map laid flat upon a table. Pauses for silence should be allowed, so that unspoken petitions can be offered.)

RESPONSE *(For use after each petition or group of petitions)*

Lord, heal us and we shall be healed.

Lord, save us and we shall be saved.

We gather together our prayers in the words that Christ taught us, and which we hold in common...... Our Father......

OFFERTORY

OFFERTORY PRAYER

Sovereign of all Creation, you who hold all things in your keeping, accept these gifts returned to you with thanksgiving, and grant that we may live our days in trust and hope, as we look for the coming of your glory amongst us. Amen.

COMMUNION HYMN *(if appropriate)*

Sovereign God, in the beginning you created us, and despite our unfaithfulness you made covenant with us, a promise which rests upon your own faithfulness and your steadfast love.

Sing praise all you nations: **Shout with joy all the earth.**

Gracious God, in Christ you came to us, showing us by your life the deeds of compassion, and through your death and resurrection the unconquerable possibilities of love.

Sing praise all you nations: **Shout with joy all the earth.**

Holy God, your presence is with us now, calling us to be holy, and to be people of wholeness for the world's healing.

Sing praise all you nations: **Shout with joy all the earth.**

(The words of the Institution of the Lord's Supper may follow here: We praise you through our Lord Jesus Christ, who on the night in which he was betrayed......)

Healing God, you are still bearing the incurable wound of the world.
It is our pain that you have taken upon yourself.
It is our burden that you carry.
It is our cross, on which you died.
It is our failure to love, our sin, our preference for the easy way that you have accepted and embraced.
And in your generosity of heart we are received, reborn, made complete, so that through us the world is made again, recreated as the realm of God, the new country of God's covenant.

Sing praise, all you nations: **Shout with joy all the earth.**

(The breaking of the bread and the distribution of the wine may follow here)

God is in our midst, we praise you as our Maker, Redeemer and Friend. Renew us and enable us to live as your covenant people for the world, this day and forever. Amen.

HYMN

BENEDICTION

May God in majesty look upon you with mercy,
May God in humility walk with you in lowliness,
May God in freedom uplift and encourage you,
from now until the close of the age. Amen.

Section 2

SEVEN SETS
OF
ADDITIONAL PRAYERS

PRAYERS OF CONFESSION AND INTERCESSION

Jesus looked at the cripple who had lain by the Pool of
Bethesda for 38 years and said:

> "Take up your bed and walk...
> give up your sinful ways."

Lord God, as we put ourselves in the shadow of your light, we
acknowledge the darkness of sin, the root of all spiritual
sickness.

> **You, Lord, are a God of forgiveness:**
> **forgive us now, we pray,**
> **and make us whole in spirit.**

Faced with the man born blind Jesus touched his eyes. First he
saw dimly, then with clear vision. Jesus sent this report of His
activities to John:

> "The blind recover their sight...
> the poor are brought good news."

Lord God, as we face the light of your truth, we see, first
dimly, and then fully the radiance of your truth.

> **You, Lord, are a God of light,**
> **heal the blindness of our spiritual eyes,**
> **that we may see your glory.**

The father brought his son to Jesus: "He has a spirit of
dumbness. It throws him about and he gets hurt." Jesus spoke
to it:

> "Deaf and dumb spirit,
> I command you, come out of him and never go back."

Lord God, we are like sheep before their shearers when we face
you, dumb creatures, hardly able to verbalise your praises.

> **You, Lord, are the God of all truth.**
> **Loosen and then govern our tongues, that we may be**
> **enabled to proclaim that truth.**

"How many of you are there?" asked Jesus of the spirits
inhabiting the Garasene demoniac. "A legion", they replied.
Jesus commanded:

> "Out, unclean spirit,
> come out of the man."

Lord, God, so often our minds are sick and we are unaware of
it, for evil brings a subtle sickness.

> **You, Lord, are the God of power.**
> **By that power, free our minds from**
> **all that makes us spiritually unhealthy.**

The man who was crippled from birth was let down through
the roof by his friends. When Jesus saw their faith He said to
the man:

> "My son, your sins are forgiven."

Lord God, we may be crippled in so many ways — in mind, body, emotions — and in turn our outlook on life and our relationships are also crippled.

> **You, Lord, have the power to**
> **straighten what is bent, to mend what**
> **is broken. Make us whole.**

The father's faith was challenged. It fell short. "I believe", he said, "help my unbelief." Jesus would eventually say:

> "Blessed are you who have not seen
> and yet have believed."

Lord God, we mar the completeness of our relationship with you by allowing doubt to brood and fester. We become imprisoned by our despairs and disappointments.

> **You, Lord, have the power to release us**
> **from these bonds and make us free.**
> **Help us to see our doubts dispelled**
> **and faith made whole today.**

The centurion came to Jesus and asked that his servant might be healed by the mere speaking of a word. Jesus was astonished.

> "Truly I tell you, nowhere in Israel have I found such faith."

Lord God, your word is sufficient for our need. Help us to understand that. But we are here, while others may only hope at a distance.

**You, Lord, have the power of healing in a
single word. You are here as you promised.
We bring to you now the names of those who cannot
be here. We may know some of their need. You know
their real needs.**

*(Names are presented by the worship leader and by members of the
congregation)*

We pray that you will pour your healing grace upon them.
May they be renewed, refreshed, and strengthened for their
journey through life.

**May they know that you are with them,
know their doubts dispelled,
their faith made whole.**

And as we who are here now come and claim your blessing in
our lives and the lives of those closest to us, may we experience
the wonder of your love and care and the deep assurance of
your peace in our lives.

Patricia Batstone

First published in *Worship and Preaching*, Vol. 21, No. 5.
October 1991

Scripture quotations from the *Revised English Bible*, 1989.

A PRAYER FOR WHOLENESS

Lord, you have made us as persons but we can differentiate
between our bodies, our minds and our spiritual capacities.
Help us to continually bind them together by a constant
awareness that you have a purpose for our total beings.

Lord, make us whole.

Lord, you gave us our bodies to be temples of the Holy Spirit.
Help us to accept responsibility for the ways in which we may
develop our physical fitness at every stage of our lives.

Lord, make us whole.

Lord, you gave us our minds that we might wrestle with the
vital issues of right and wrong, truth and falsehood.
Grant us your help in order to use our minds to penetrate to
the heart of reality and to discern your mind, especially in tight
corners.

Lord, make us whole,

Lord, you gave us our inward spiritual beings together with the
ability to become joined to you, spirit to Spirit. Help us to use
this precious gift to tune in constantly to the music of your
wisdom.

Lord, make us whole.

So, Lord, we are one as persons but also a trinity of our
bodies, minds and spiritual capacities. Grant us the maturity to
co-operate with your purposes so that all three aspects of being
may unite to your glory.

Lord, make us whole through the wholeness we find, day by day, in the one truly whole person, your Son, our Saviour, Jesus Christ.

AMEN.

LIGHTEN OUR DARKNESS

A form of prayer for the closing of the day at a week-end residential conference.

(Those present are invited to make a circle around a low table on which is placed a cross and a lighted candle. All other lights are switched off or dimmed. Soft music is being played as the people assemble.)

Light and peace are in Jesus Christ our Lord.
Thanks be to God.

From the rising of the sun to the going down of the same.
The Lord's name be praised.

You, O Lord are our lamp.
Make our darkness bright.

Hold us together in Christ
So that we may lighten each other's burdens.

Grant us, O Lord, a peaceful evening.
Watch over us while we sleep.

Glory be to the Father and to the Son and to the Holy Spirit.
As it was in the beginning, is now, and shall be for ever.

AMEN

HYMN: At even when the sun was set

Read Psalm 4 'Night Prayer'. *(See the Meditation built around this Psalm in the 'Psalm Meditations', Section 4, page 106, of this Worship Book)*

CARING AND SHARING

(Invite those present to tell of something that has happened to them either recently or during the conference. Ask that these sharing moments be interspersed with short prayers for themselves or for others, both present and absent. Make it clear that silence is not failure nor should we be concerned about long periods of quiet. God can use the quietness as well as the spoken words. Let this be a time of helpful relaxation 'in the Lord'. Quiet Choruses could also be sung such as 'Spirit of the Living God', 'Jesus we adore you, lay our lives before you' and 'Turn your eyes upon Jesus'.)

CLOSING PRAYERS

For this day together; for its friendship, inspiration and blessing; for new thoughts and fresh resolves...
We bless the Lord.

For this place in which we meet, for those who have made us welcome, prepared our food and made us feel at home...
We bless the Lord.

For our church(es) and those whom we have left behind; for their care for us and their prayers for our well-being...
We bless the Lord.

For our families, absent and present; for all that they give to us and for the privilege of giving ourselves to them...
We bless the Lord.

We pray for the end results of this conference; for any who have been touched and blessed; that the future may be different because of discoveries made. Lord, if any have been disappointed and if anyone has felt lonely, grant them a special blessing and may we love them wisely. Help us to be our true selves and to help one another to find our real selves. Lord, someone may want to offer a special prayer at this particular stage as we draw our worship to a close...

(Further short opportunity for personal prayers — spoken or unspoken)

HYMN: Glory to Thee my God this night

**Lighten our darkness we beseech thee, O Lord,
And by thy good pleasure defend us from all the perils of this night,
Through the love of thine only Son, our Lord and Saviour Jesus Christ.   Amen.**

(Suggest that all share 'The Peace' and then go quietly to bed without further conversation)

PRAYERS FOR HEALING AND RECONCILIATION

> But for you who fear my Name the sun of
> righteousness shall rise with healing
> in its wings.
>
> *(Malachi 4:2)*

God promises his healing power to those who love and trust
Him.

We come now to acknowledge that promise and to claim that
power of healing in our lives, in our church, in our world.

> Lord, through your power
> **Heal us today.**

★　★　★　★　★

> All this is from God, who through Christ
> reconciled us to himself and gave us the
> ministry of reconciliation.
>
> *(2 Corinthians 5:18)*

Healing involves so many areas of our lives, not least our
relationships with one another, in our homes, in the community
and especially in the fellowship of the church.

Where we have fallen short in our relationship, we come now
seeking reconciliation through the love of Jesus by whom all
may be reconciled and be as one.

68

Lord, in your love
May we be as one.

★ ★ ★ ★ ★

(Jesus') fame spread... and they brought Him all the sick, those afflicted with various diseases and pain, demoniacs, epileptics, and paralytics, and He healed them.

(Matthew 4:24)

Bodily healing is always uppermost in our minds, for that is healing which enables us to be fully functioning in our daily lives. God uses many means for our healing, from the skill of the surgeon to the touch of a hand in prayer.

We now come seeking that healing through the ministry of hands and hearts.

Lord, in your power
Heal us, we pray.

★ ★ ★ ★ ★

Jesus... went about doing good and healing all that were oppressed by the devil, for God was with Him.

(Acts 10:38)

Mental and emotional sickness are harder to contain than the physical. Life becomes one dark tunnel of oppression and depression and the forces of evil weigh heavily upon us. But God is with us there in that tunnel, and His power is greater than the forces that are arrayed against us.

We come now to claim God's overcoming power in times of depression and overwhelming anxiety.

> Lord, in your goodness
> **Deliver us, we pray.**

★ ★ ★ ★ ★

> Beloved, I pray that all may go well with you
> and that you may be in health;
> I know that it is well with your soul.
>
> *(3 John 2)*

The greatest and most important area of healing for the Christian is that of the spirit. If we are right with God we know that He will never leave us without the strength to overcome all the threats to our health that the world may inflict upon us.

We come now, seeking God's will for our lives, committing ourselves to him, regardless of cost, confident in his saving grace and loving care for our souls.

> Lord, in your grace
> **Guide us, we pray.**

★ ★ ★ ★ ★

> When he had spoken to me... I turned my face towards
> the ground and was dumb. And behold, one in the
> likeness of the sons of men touched my lips; then I
> opened my mouth and spoke. I said to him who stood
> before me, "O my lord, by reason of the vision

pains have come upon me, and I retain no strength. How can my lord's servant talk with my lord? For no strength remains in me, and no breath is left in me".

Again one having the appearance of a man touched me and strengthened me. And he said, "O man greatly beloved, fear not, peace be with you; be strong and of good courage". And when he spoke to me, I was strengthened and said, "Let my lord speak, for you have strengthened me".   *(Daniel 10:15-19)*

With healing will come peace — peace in our hearts, peace in our minds, peace in our bodies, and, at peace within ourselves, we are at peace with our surroundings and with our colleagues in work and worship. He makes us strong enough to overcome.

As we draw our thoughts together, we look for peace in our lives, in our church, in our troubled world.

    Lord, in your mercy
    Grant us your peace.

       ★   ★   ★   ★   ★

And so, with the prophet Jeremiah, we affirm:

Heal me, O Lord, and I shall be healed,
save me and I shall be saved. *(17:14)*

We pray not only for ourselves but for others in need of healing:

    (Names may be mentioned by the worship
    leader and members of the congregation)

71

So Father, we lift up these our brothers and sisters to you and pray that your grace shall meet their every need and your strength shall be made perfect in weakness.

AMEN.

by Patricia Batstone (slightly amended)

All scripture quotations are from the Revised Standard Version of the Bible.

PRAYING ABOUT STRESS

(There is nothing intrinsically evil or bad about stress. It is necessary for our development and growth as persons. The problem is what happens to us when we are subjected to the stress factor. It is then that what we are as persons will be revealed. If problems emerge like exhaustion, lack of concentration, bad temper, this need not necessarily lead on to further complications and illness. When the adverse consequences of stress are recognised, then is the time to do something about it. There are courses on stress management and there are many books, one of which is recommended below.

But should we pray about stress? Might this seem to be the easy option which could in fact complicate the whole situation and, indeed, make matters worse?

We certainly should pray about stress. We are told by Jesus to love ourselves (Mark 12:31). Therefore it follows that prayer for ourselves is both legitimate and has divine sanction. However the old adage, "God helps those who help themselves" is relevant here. Our prayer should facilitate our search for help and be complementary to it. The nature of our praying should also relate to our growing understanding of the nature of our problems. The prayers outlined here could be used in a health and healing service about stress or on other occasions with an introductory explanation. The Service we have entitled 'In Quietness and Confidence' in Section 6, page 168, is one in which these prayers could be used.)

★ ★ ★ ★ ★

73

A PRAYER FOR GROWING SELF-AWARENESS

O Lord, show us ourselves. Help us to be open with ourselves, realistic and honest. As now we spend time in quiet with you and with each other, we ask you to guide our exploration.

> Help each one of us by laying your hand upon the root of our anxiety.

> *(Quiet)*

> Remind us that you love us just as we are.

> *(Quiet)*

> Now may we feel your hand moving in the dark corners of our inward lives, deeply probing but with loving care.

> *(Quiet)*

> Show us gently what we need to know.

> *(Quiet)*

> Assure us that you are now in those dark corners with us and will always be so, and that your presence will bring light and hope.

> *(Quiet)*

Lord, we thank you; we trust you; we rest in your gracious provision. Take us on from here. In Jesus' name.   Amen.

★ ★ ★ ★ ★

A PRAYER OF CONFESSION

Lord, each one of us simply wants to talk with you. We want to share ourselves with you. We are sorry that we are as we are and can't explain it. We don't want to be like this; we want to be inwardly strong and able to cope.

Those areas of failure in our lives of which we are conscious, we confess to you.

(In the quietness, be specific)

Those areas of need in our lives of which we are aware we bring to you.

(In the quietness, be specific)

Remind us that you have promised always your gracious forgiveness and the added bonus that in our weakness we shall find strength.

(Quietness)

For all that you are now doing for us; for the greater sense of inner well-being we are already feeling, we give you thanks.

(In the quietness, be thankful)

In Jesus' name. Amen.

A PRAYER JOURNEY INTO SPACE

Lord, you have given us the precious gift of time. We are not
in any hurry; we just want to spend time with you and have
space to breathe and be ourselves. In our first period of prayer
we are simply going to breathe deeply, relax and enjoy
our bodies.

(Simple breathing/relaxation)

Now, Lord we are going to explore our feelings and we
are going to express them to you, whatever they are.

(Tell God exactly how you feel — don't hide anything)

Now we bring our minds to you; we want to develop our
thinking powers and live on a larger map. Show us how
and, whilst we continue to live in the real world, fill
our minds with good things. *(Philippians 4:8)*

(Dwell on the Bible words)

And now Lord we ask for the blessing which binds all
the other of your gifts together, spiritual wisdom and
insight into your positive plan for each of our lives.
We have asked you to show us ourselves, now Lord we
ask, *show us Thyself.*

(Let go and let God)

Amen

A PRAYER OF THANKSGIVING

Our Father we thank you through Jesus Christ, for your direct personal interest in our lives. We are grateful for our growing confidence both in you and in ourselves. That which you are giving us we treasure and we desire it for itself, but also that we may be more useful instruments in your service. Take us on from here, Lord, and give us the wisdom to realise that, from time to time we may fall back, but that we shall always rise up again and move on. Praise be to you Father, Son and Holy Spirit. Amen.

Notes:

1.   The recommended book is *At Ease with Stress* by Wanda Nash, published by Darton, Longman and Todd.

2.   Apart from the Prayer of Thanksgiving the above prayers could last at least 5 to 10 minutes each, giving proper time for reflective thought. The leader will sense when real business with God is taking place and act accordingly.

3.   It would be especially appropriate to use the above in connection with a retreat.

PRAYING WHICH MAKES A DIFFERENCE

*(All those who conduct and lead worship have a heavy
responsibility. There is a tendency sometimes to think of worship as
a performance. Comments made after some services to the leaders or
celebrants reinforce this: "We have had a good time, this morning";
"Thank you for holding my interest — I didn't have my usual
nap!" All very nice, but the purpose of worship is primarily to help
people to make God-contact; to feel that they are furthering their
relationship with God and actually doing business with Him. One
of the best ways is to offer stimulation to the people to enter into the
times of prayer by putting their whole selves into what is
happening. This does not usually happen when the congregation has
a passive role. Nor does it always happen if a liturgical response is
suggested. What follows is a series of suggestions to put before a
congregation with again — and I make no apologies for this —
significant periods of silence. Our aim is not just to pray on behalf
of others, but to enable others — and ourselves — really to pray.
Here is a suggested pattern for stimulating prayer with a difference
which, hopefully, will make a difference to those who participate.)*

1.   DISCOVER QUIET DEEP INSIDE OURSELVES

a)   Get rid of physical tension — simple relaxation exercises.
*(These can happen without any fuss or awkwardness — see 'In
Quietness and Confidence' in Section 6, page 168.)*

b)   Pray the scriptures — "Let the word of Christ, in all its
richness, find a home in you". *(Col:3:16)* Use a simple verse
from the Bible and allow your mind to wander imaginatively
around it but always keep applying what you find to your own
needs. Or do the same with a single word which Jesus applied

to himself like Light, Shepherd, Door, Way. Take a scripture story and turn it into a personal prayer. The woman looking for a piece of silver in Luke 15 can be the basis of a prayer for your own desire to recover lost enthusiasm, lost spiritual vitality.

c) Offer your simple responses to God and seal them by deciding what practical steps you are going to take to facilitate your own developing Christian life.

2. BE GRATEFUL FOR MYSTERY

a) A problem may be thought of as a knot in life. The untying of a knot can be the means of opening up a door into the riches of mystery, but mystery remains and often cannot be analysed. It can however be appreciated and enjoyed. (ie the mystery of what actually happens in the Service of Holy Communion, when, as we sometimes say, we celebrate the 'Holy Mysteries'.)

b) Remember — "Canst thou by searching find out God?" (*Job 11:7*)

— "It is the glory of God to conceal a thing". (*Proverbs 25:2*)

— "Great is the mystery of godliness" (*1 Tim 3:16*)

c) Give thanks for mystery but give thanks also for those shafts of light that come from Jesus and remember that although now "we see through a mirror darkly, one day we shall see face to face". (*1 Corinthians 13:12*)

3. ACCEPT THAT GOD WANTS TO BRING YOU CLOSER TO HIM

a) Here is an actual testimony: "The whole direction of my life has changed. The first half of my life was about what I could do for God. The latter half has been centred upon what God is trying to do for me."

b) Another testimony: "My ideal was once to dedicate myself to God and other people, now the starting point has moved a step further back — to accepting and appreciating first of all, God's love in everything and everyone".

c) Yet another: "Private prayer has become the opening up of that inner self to God — a time for listening and receiving. And liturgy has become a celebration of thanksgiving. Gratitude overflows in a fuller enjoyment of every aspect of life."

How does the nature of these testimonies challenge your own stage of Christian development? Are there aspects of the testimonies which surprise you?

4. OUR RESPONSE TO GOD

a) Praise God for your growing ability to discover inner quiet. Ask for his help if you feel you need special grace to enable you to find real quietness within.

b) Praise God for mystery, including the 'Holy Mysteries'. Thank God for every flash of light; for every simple, yet profound insight into mystery, which comes to you.

c) Praise God for new understanding of the real meaning of life in Christ.

Here is what Mother Teresa says... "Unless we change our hearts we are not converted. Changing places is not the answer. Changing occupations is not the answer. The answer is to change our hearts. And how do we change? By praying."

PRAYING WITH OUR BODIES

*(Our bodies are the most obvious part of us; the means whereby we
are recognised. Before people begin to think deeply about the
personality of someone they are talking about, they conjure up a
visual image of their physical likeness. Our bodies frequently express
what is happening within our minds, our emotions, our spirits.
Being sad, frustrated, bored, happy, angry, all these soon show
themselves in bodily form. It is possible to become fanatical about
physical fitness and respond to every new exercise technique and
dietary fad. This lack of balance in some people's approach to their
bodies should not lead us to neglect our own bodies — or other
people's for that matter. Can we pray with our bodies? The answer
is that we cannot pray without them. We are persons and if we are
to be on the way towards becoming whole persons, we must pay
attention to our bodies. Praying with our bodies can help us here.
The following suggestions are for a prayer/meditation which could
be used privately or in a group or with a willing congregation.
I stress the word 'willing' because no congregation should be asked
to do unusual things without being fully prepared and
given the opportunity to opt out.)*

★ ★ ★ ★ ★

Do you not know that your body is a temple of the Holy Spirit
within you? Glorify God in your body.

(1 Corinthians 6:19-20)

> As the body is clothed in cloth
> and the muscles in the skin
> and the bones in the muscles
> and the heart in the chest,
> so are we, body and soul,

clothed in the goodness of God
and enclosed.

God is the means
whereby our substance
and our sensuality
are kept together
so as to be never apart.

(From the Meditations of Julian of Norwich)

1.   *As you enjoy your simple relaxation exercises (see 'In Quietness
and Confidence' in Section 6, page 168) and move slowly up your
body, give God thanks for each part. Touch each part if you feel it
appropriate and recognise its value and worth. Recall the
importance of each part of the body co-operating with the other.*

Under his control all the different parts
of the body fit together, and the whole body is held
together by every joint with which it is provided. So
when each separate part works as it should, the whole
body grows and builds itself up through love.

(Ephesians 4:16)

Yes, Paul is here referring to the unity of the church but the
analogy he uses is that of the body and the way he uses it fits
perfectly into our pattern of thinking here. Note especially the
final statement, "the whole body grows and builds itself up
through love". Feel yourself being embraced by God's love.
Allow yourself to be 'cuddled' and comforted.

2. *Reflect on how the everyday activities of life can be the means of praying with our bodies:*

a) Enjoy washing, bathing, showering. Feel the cleansing effects of water. Appreciate the effects of both warm and cold water. Warmth for comfort; cold for challenge. Let the spray from the shower dance all over you and and enjoy the sheer exhilaration. Cultivate the feeling that you are being cleansed inwardly as well as outwardly.

b) Enjoy eating. Eat slowly and sense the smell and feel the texture of what you are eating. Revel in the tastes you enjoy. Take sips of beverages and taste well before swallowing. If it seems natural to do so relate all this to the Holy Eucharist. Recall the preciousness of some sacramental experiences. Begin to see and feel every meal as a Sacrament. After all the first celebrations of Holy Communion took place at the ordinary, everyday meal table.

c) Enjoy walking. Choose to walk rather than ride. Feel the value of your legs as they carry you along. Place your feet down firmly in secure places. Let your arms move and take note of the sights and sounds around you.

> O for a closer walk with God,
> A calm and heavenly frame,
> A light to shine upon the road,
> That leads me to the Lamb.   *(William Cowper)*

Walk in love.   *(Ephesians 5:2)*

Walk as children of the light.   *(Ephesians 5:8)*

Walk carefully.   *(Ephesians 5:15)*

3.   *In actual prayer times link the body with the use of your imagination.*

When I used to share in leading retreats for ordinands I invited them to use time during retreat to prepare an imaginary room into which they could enter amid all the excitement and sound of the ordination service. The nature of the room and its furnishing could be determined, stage by stage, during the retreat. It would include a place on the wall for an account of their initial call to the ministry. It would have places in the room for the members of their family. Key books would be on the shelves. Vital decisions contained in a prayer diary on the desk. It was to be a room in which they could truly be themselves. Many spoke to me in appreciation of the suggestion and some kept the room vision as an ongoing part of their daily experience.

a)   You have such a room and you are in it now. The room is full of light. Let that light permeate to every part of you. Raise your arms to pull down the light so that it gets nearer and nearer. Light does two things — among others — shows the way and shows up the dirt. Ask for both blessings, and go on to ask for the way to be clear and for the dirt to be cleansed. But don't try to hide from the fact that it is real dirt. Help the cleansing process by giving God a hand with the broom (or the vacuum cleaner!).

b)   Have objects near to you which remind you of special places. (I have stones from the Holy Land and the top of Ben Nevis; shells from Iona; photographs of Corrymeela.) They help me to be there. I can feel my body experiencing those delights and pleasures. I can return to what those places meant to me. The stones can be moved from hand to hand; the shells placed to the ear; the photographs can be touched as well as looked at.

c) Get into the habit of touching leaves and plants. Feel
yourself drawing strength from the plants. They have a life of
their own but you can share it. Do the same with the branches
of trees and see the broken branches lying on the ground.
Recall the parable of the vine and the branches in John 15. As
you touch the trunk feel yourself touching the very source of
life and spiritual power — none other than Jesus himself.

End all these bodily experiences with praise and thanksgiving.
You have been making use of God's creation. He is "Alpha and
Omega, the beginning and the end". He is Creator, Sustainer,
and although our world, universe and space are all his, he has
come to us in Jesus and shown himself. With every part of you
— GIVE THANKS!

★ ★ ★ ★ ★

NOTE

Those who lead such exercises in which the physical body
figures prominently should always be mindful of the feelings of
disabled people who may feel some aspects of what is suggested
above to be hurtful. Yet experience has shown that where there
is careful explanation no hurt is felt. Indeed many disabled
people have spoken of the value of affirming their bodily parts
even when they may be limited in their mobility and are
perhaps scarred and disfigured. This is the experience of Jean
Vanier with those belonging to l'Arche communities all over the
world. We conclude this section with his words:

...my brother, my sister,
do not run away from people in pain
or who are broken,
but walk towards them,
touch them.
Then you will find rising up within you
the well of love,
springing from resurrection.

Joy springs from the wounds of brokenness
and Jesus is hidden in the poor, the weak,
the lonely and the oppressed.

(The Broken Body)

Acknowledgement: Some of the ideas in this section
were suggested by Flora Slosson
Wueller in her book, *Prayer and Our
Bodies* (The Upper Room, USA.)

Section 3

SEVEN HYMNS

BEYOND MEASURE

We cannot measure how you heal
Or answer every sufferer's prayer,
Yet we believe your grace responds
Where faith and doubt unite to care.
Your hands, though bloodied by the cross,
Survive to hold and heal and warn,
To carry all through death to life
And cradle children yet unborn.

The pain that will not go away,
The guilt that clings from things long past,
The fear of what the future holds,
Are present as if meant to last.
But present too is love which tends
The hurt we never hoped to find,
The private agonies inside,
The memories that haunt the mind.

So some have come who need your help
And some have come to make amends,
As hands which shaped and saved the world
Are present in the touch of friends.
Lord, let your Spirit meet us here
To mend the body, mind and soul,
To disentangle peace from pain
And make your broken people whole.

J. Bell and G. Maule

Written to be sung to the traditional Scottish tune *Ye Banks and Braes.*

A HYMN FOR HEALING SERVICES

Jesus, the healer, come to us, we pray;
We long for your touch every hour of the day,
We do not dictate what your coming may mean,
But just want you actively here on the scene.

Jesus, you know how we long to be well,
Some people such stories of healings do tell:
While others are prayed for and they are not healed,
Compounding the sense of frustration we feel.

Our needs are so complex, we cannot discern,
How best you can help us, but please let us learn
That your gracious bonding of each of our parts,
Makes healing begin by renewing our hearts.

Our need is for wholeness; of this we are sure,
Of all of our longings, this is the most pure;
So give us the vision which helps us to see,
In searching and trusting, you give us the key.

Jesus, the healer, come to us, we pray,
Give your guiding grace for each step of the way,
Secure in this knowledge, may we find our peace,
Just knowing your love for us never will cease.

Can be sung to the tune Slane (Metre 10 11.11.12)

Howard Booth

A HYMN FOR COUNSELLORS

Jesus, your love I know,
Give me the grace to grow;
May I thus enabled be,
Others wounds to clearly see:
Guide me to their deepest need,
So that I may sow good seed.

Jesus, I safely stand,
Held firm by your good hand;
This is my security,
Give me sensitivity:
So that those who come to share,
Feel that I do truly care.

Jesus, you showed the way,
The price you had to pay;
Those who come to me feel lost,
Help me now to bear the cost:
Give me wisdom from above,
Patience, understanding, love.

Jesus, you came to save,
Sins freely you forgave;
Needy people came to life,
Delivered from their inner strife:
May I Lord, your channel be,
Helping others to be free.

Can be sung to the tune Devotion (Metre 66.7.7.7.7)

Howard Booth

THE WOUNDED HEALER

His wounds are healing wounds;
Which show his love for me.
They penetrate my inward heart:
"All this I did for thee".

My wounds are part of me,
Healed now, though scars remain;
Forgiven hurts enable me,
Reach others in their pain.

Come, be my welcome guest,
My heart is open wide;
Re-live your hurts in confidence,
The Lord is on your side.

Then go your way in peace,
Your wounds and His combine,
To progress your discipleship,
And cause the sun to shine.

Can be sung to the tune Franconia (Short Metre)

Howard Booth

SHALOM

Shalom, Shalom, the gift of God above;
The gift of peace and joy and life and love.

Lord, give us peace, the peace that makes us whole,
The peace that fills the heart and mind and soul.

Lord, give us joy, the joy that comes from Thee,
Found in completeness and security.

Lord, give us life, the life from God above;
Wholeness of being, blessedness and love.

Lord, give us love, the love that sets us free;
To work for others and to live for Thee.

Shalom, Shalom, God's gift is thus assured —
They shall find peace who wait upon the Lord.

Ivor Pearce

Can be sung to the tune Pax Tecum (Metre 10.10)

PRAYER FOR HEALING

Here, Master in this quiet place,
Where anyone can kneel,
I also come to ask for grace,
Believing you can heal.

If pain of body, stress of mind,
Destroys my inward peace,
In prayer for others, may I find
The secret of release.

If self upon its sickness feeds
And turns my life to gall,
Let me not brood upon my needs,
But simply tell you all.

You never said "you ask too much"
To any troubled soul.
I long to feel your healing touch,
Will you not make me whole?

But if the thing I most desire,
Is not your way for me,
May faith, when tested in the fire,
Prove its integrity.

Of all my prayers, may this be chief:
Till faith is fully grown,
Lord, disbelieve my unbelief,
And claim me as your own.

F. Pratt Green

CHRIST'S CALL

Christ's call to us to heal the sick
Crosses all bounds of time and place,
The whole world is his Galilee,
His patients all the human race.

Grant us, O Christ, your tender heart,
Your listening ear, perceptive mind,
To welcome those who suffer hurt,
That here they may your healing find.

We come in faith, your power is such,
That minds relieved from stress and fear,
And bodies quickened by your touch,
Shall own you Lord, your name revere.

Meet with us now, dear loving Lord,
Healer of body, mind and soul,
Speak to our hearts your living word,
Revive, restore, and make us whole.

Stanley Smith

Can be sung to the tune Fulda (Long Metre)

Section 4

SEVEN MEDITATIONS
BASED ON
SEVEN PSALMS

Introduction

The Bible, taken collectively, is the word of God to man. The Psalms, taken separately, can be described as the words of man to God. The Psalms raise questions with God in a variety of different ways. They also record God's answers but not in an absolute and definitive way like the Ten Commandments or the Beatitudes. The messages contained in the Psalms are devotional. The same questions are asked, often in different forms, again and again. The answers relate to the different circumstances in which the questions were asked.

In his commentary on the Psalms Calvin expressed it in this way:

> The varied and resplendent riches which are contained in this treasury it is no easy matter to express in words... I have been accustomed to call this book, not inappropriately, 'An Anatomy of all the parts of the Soul'; for there is not an emotion of which anyone can be conscious that is not represented here as in a mirror.

This says it all. Every emotion — praise, thanksgiving, sorrow, penitence, anger, rage, guilt, trust, hope — they are all here in the Psalms.

The Psalms were written before the time of Christ but we read them with the added benefit of Christ's revelation. Therefore we put into the Psalms elements of truth that have come to us in Christ but which fit simply and properly into what the Psalmist is saying. This is quite in order seeing that the Book of Psalms stands alone in scripture as a book of worship and devotion. By tradition the Psalms are not used as Bible lessons but like hymns as the vehicle of worship. So, for contemporary

Christians, the Psalms have been set 'in Christ' from the very beginning. So the Lord who is our Shepherd in Psalm 23 is Jesus and he is also the Good Shepherd whom Jesus claimed to be. This happens again and again but in different contexts. Thus the Psalms have been captured for Christ and are an extension of his ministry.

So the Psalms provide abundant material for reflection; for the use of guided imagination, and as a means whereby we express our own feelings, longings, desires and resolves. They will stir, challenge, comfort and disturb us but, above all, they will bring us closer to God.

These seven Psalms will, I hope, show us that it is possible to use the Psalms with imagination in relation to today's needs and opportunities. However they only scratch the surface of what it is possible to obtain from this well-stocked treasury.

These meditations were first used during a special week at Willersley Castle in July 1992. After an appropriate hymn the expository part was used as a devotional introduction. The meditation sentences were then spoken slowly against the background of quiet Taizé chants or classical guitar music.

THE TWO WAYS   Psalm 1

> To every soul there openeth,
> a way, and ways, and the way.
> And the high soul takes the high way,
> and the low soul gropes the low,
> and in between, on the misty flats
> the rest drift to and fro.
>
> But to every soul there openeth
> a high way and a low,
> and every soul decideth
> the way his soul shall go.
>
> *(Author unknown)*

When the Book of Psalms had been compiled the Editors decided to write an Introduction. This is quite usual today. It is only when the book is complete that the author or editor knows how he or she wants to introduce it to the readers. In the case of the Book of Psalms, the introduction is Psalm 1. It is this Psalm which sets out the basic stance of the whole book: there are two possible ways we can all go; these exist in stark simplicity as God's way and the way of those who reject God.

1. The Psalmist describes three possible stages of deterioration: first, simply ceasing to believe; then blatantly ignoring God's laws; finally becoming a 'scornful' man who has no time for anyone but himself — he even scoffs at those who are trying to find and follow God's way.

2. In order to be blessed, however, there is a better way: it is to ponder on the words of the Lord, holding them firmly in

our minds and letting them filter down into the deepest part of our beings.

3.   The fruitful tree is a symbol frequently used in the Bible to describe a meaningful God-centred life. The word *planted* and the phrase *by rivers of water* are both full of meditative suggestions. It is the gardener who plants; thus it is God who takes the initiative. To be placed in *good soil* and sited near *rivers of water* is to belong to a caring fellowship of people who, individually and collectively, provide channels of grace.

The consequences of such a life need always to be explored. Taken at their face value it is material success and worldly prosperity which are being suggested. This is an illustration of where the Psalms need always to be *Christed*; ie baptised into Christ. In him prosperity often means something quite different. It is life in which God's grace proves to be sufficient and where strength is provided in times of weakness (see 2 Corinthians 12:9.)

4.   'Bitty' lives have no calm centre. Such people rush about and are always in a hurry — but they get nowhere. In the final analysis it is the mature, wounded souls who survive.

5.   When people appeared before Aslan the Lion in *The Narnia Tales* by C.S. Lewis, some looked into his eyes and turned away in fear; others looked and were content. There is a judgement day but God does not condemn us; we condemn ourselves.

6.   So goodness is its own reward. The key word is *knoweth* or *know*. There is often a deep awareness of God in the hearts and lives of those who love him which goes beyond intellectual assent.

MEDITATION

Just how do we get God's truth down into the very centre of our being?

Visualise an oasis in the scorching desert with pure water and fruit for your refreshment. God makes adequate provision for all our needs. Do we sometimes neglect it?

He is the still point of the turning world.

The Lord is on your side. He wants you to walk with him.

There are two possible ways ahead for you. Travel along them both in your mind and imagination. Along one of them you will feel at peace with God and at ease with yourself. This is the way for you — and it is the way of Jesus.

NIGHT PRAYER   Psalm 4

Karen (not her real name) suffered with insomnia. She did
not like taking sleeping pills and her doctor did not like
prescribing them for one so young. Karen had prayed a great
deal about her problem and her doctor (a personal friend)
spoke to me, her minister, about her needs.

The doctor's practical suggestions were a warm milky drink last
thing at night plus a brisk walk 'round the houses'. Also she
should avoid taking any 'naps' during the day.

I began to help Karen with practical relaxation exercises. We
decided that she should stop praying directly about going to
sleep at night but that she would gather helpful thoughts from
the Bible and other books for her to hold in her mind. We
recorded some of these on tape and Karen could then use her
'Walkman' when she was in bed without disturbing anyone else
in the house.

Slowly our joint efforts — Karen's, her doctor's and mine,
began to bear fruit. By not fighting her problem but seeking to
engage in diversionary tactics, progress was made. Karen also
said that her Christian life was becoming more real. One of the
passages we used was this Psalm. Appropriately it is called
Night Prayer.

1. At night we are often at our lowest. This is particularly so
during times of illness and physical weakness. The person who
wrote this Psalm had previously experienced God's faithfulness
and he longed for this to be repeated. He did believe that God
was just and wanted him to prove this in his current dilemma.

2.   He now turns to think of those who are troubling him. He is anxious for their welfare but feels that they must change their ways.

3. The idea that prosperity follows upon goodness is often expressed in the Psalms. This Psalm seems to suggest that "the Lord looks after his own". But in what ways? Those who put their trust in God have often suffered and died in great adversity. Yet within that adversity they have found strength and through it character and personality have been developed. As Julian of Norwich put it "our wounds can become our worships".

4.   There are two different kinds of anger. The first is anger which is created by becoming aware of injustice and sheer inequality. This was the kind of anger that stimulated General William Booth to become the founder of the Salvation Army and young Dr. Barnardo to begin his great work for neglected children. The anger which is plain sin is anger which is generated because we feel affronted; we are not getting our own way. This kind of anger will disturb our sleep and deserves to do so.

What is it that enables us to commune with God deep in our own hearts? How can we discover that inner silence which is the gateway to sound sleep? Surely the answer lies in the ways we discipline our thought life — the books we read — the television programmes we watch. This does not mean opting out of the real world. It does mean exercising control over our phantasies.

5.   Offering 'right sacrifices' relates to the cultic acts which prevailed at the time this Psalm was written. As we shall see in a later study "the sacrifice acceptable to God is a broken spirit; a broken and a contrite heart" (Psalm 51:17).

6,7.   Here is the heart and kernel of this Psalm. People look for satisfaction in the wrong places — abundant supplies of food and wine. There are greater joys to be found in simpler life-styles and in caring service.

8.   So sleep comes. Good sleep. Sound sleep. We are safe, secure, enfolded in love. It doesn't come easily but we can make slow and steady progress every day.

MEDITATION

Think about how your past experiences of God's goodness have helped you in times of trial.

What is your attitude towards those who you think are acting unhelpfully towards you? Think of an actual situation. What positive action could you take?

In what ways do you try to feed your mind so that you have a rich store of creativity on which to draw?

George Matheson wrote about "Joy seeking him through pain" and seeing "the rainbow through the rain".

When Job was in deep distress the only light that came to him was when he "saw the Lord". Ask specifically to "see the Lord" in your own situation.

What are your own practices last thing at night before you retire? Do you wind down and prepare for a good night's sleep by drawing upon helpful 'night thoughts' before you sleep?

HE LEADETH ME   Psalm 23

There is no Psalm more loved and quoted than this one. Why
is this? First it is simple and full of imaginative detail. Then it
is directly honest and true to life. The existence of the shadows
is properly recognised. Indeed it is because of the shadows that
we become more acutely aware of the sunshine.

Once I was at Minsteracres Monastery and Retreat Centre in
the North East. One sunny afternoon I stood alone at the
entrance to a glorious, wide path bordered by giant
Wellingtonian trees. Their great trunks soared up into the
heights and their leaves and branches formed arches making the
whole scene like some vast, outdoor cathedral. The sun shone
brightly but the great trees cast their shadows before me. It
was a time of vision. The sun would not have seemed so bright
were it not being seen against the background of the shadows.

In this combination of delight in simple things and robust
acceptance of the existence of the shadows lies this Psalm's
greatness. Life is not all enjoyment. Characters are being made
and real persons developed when there has to be honest
grappling with the darkness. The key to the ability to do so lies
in our renewing experiences in the green pastures and beside
the still waters.

1.   The Shepherd endeavours to provide adequately for his
flock but sometimes there may be experiences of want. The
recent experiences of the hostages illustrates this. Even when in
dire straits some small and trivial occurrence delivered them
from utter despair. Nevertheless God's people must always be
in the vanguard of movements to promote justice and an equal
sharing of material blessings.

2. He *maketh* me to lie down. Often this is true. We come to a
point in life when we are compelled to rest; illness or other
circumstances demand it.

3. Note that the process of strengthening is prior to the test.
Rest then, is for re-charging the batteries to face the next
challenge. The middle and later years of life invite a gradual
separation from dependence upon material things and earthly
pleasures. They are still enjoyed but we do not entirely rely
upon them for our contentment.

4. The valley may well be both deep and long. From time to
time we shall feel the gentle touch of the restraining rod but
the Shepherd will also give us the loan of his staff. Sometimes
it is necessary for God to remind us that we are going astray.
Sometimes he may even let us stray in order that the wounding
experience might assist our growth and development.

5. Here the symbolism changes and the Shepherd becomes the
Host. The emphasis is now on a different but related form of
provision. The table is for feeding; on it lies our sustenance
and it is for the refreshment of weary travellers. Anointing with
oil has become related to healing, The imagination can soon
connect this with the adequate provision made at the Lord's
Table where we receive... "a foretaste of the heavenly banquet
prepared for all mankind".

6. Life is a journey and to every journey there is the time of
arrival — journey's end. The journey and its climax are closely
related: "the everlasting life 'tis here and now" (Percy
Ainsworth — *Poems and Sonnets*). Enjoyed in the present, it
will not be unfamiliar in the future. God's love will ensure our
final completion, our complete wholeness, our ultimate healing.

MEDITATION

Recall a time when you experienced special grace in
time of need. Who or what brought the help you
needed? Re-live your thankfulness.

Visualise deep, still waters, calm and unruffled by wind.
See a deep carpet of restful green.
Let go and let God.
Rest does not mean stagnation. It is for renewal and
refreshment.
Then — where He leads, follow.

God's renewing activity invites our co-operation. It is a
privilege to work in harmony with the great creator —
'through all the changing scenes of life'.

When were you last blessed by feeling the application of
the restraining rod?

What feelings and thoughts do you associate with the
service of Holy Communion? Have you ever
contemplated seeking to be anointed with oil?

Are you enjoying your pilgrimage?

With what confidence do you face the ending of your
earthly journey?

DEALING WITH MOODS   Psalm 42

All of us know what it is to move from one mood to another.
We wake up full of anticipation for the day that lies ahead.
Then something happens which triggers an unhappy incident
from the past or brings an unresolved conflict into our
conscious memory — and we sink down into the depths.
Sometimes the causes of our moods lie buried in the
unconscious so, for us, they are inexplicable.

The question is not how we avoid moods; they are part of the
stuff of life. In a very real sense we need them in order that we
might practice dealing with them in positive ways. However, as
we turn to this Psalm for help for ourselves, let us not forget
those for whom depressive experiences are a regular part of
everyday living. (We may even be such people ourselves.) For
these there are no easy, simple solutions and they may require
skilled help. At the same time there is hope for all as this
Psalm with its realism and honesty indicates.

1-2.   This vivid picture of the exhausted animal seeking
refreshment from a flowing stream and finding only a dried
up river bed has burnt itself into the mind of the Psalmist.
Now he is in the same position: thirsty and longing for the
satisfaction of meaningful communion with God. Did he (I
can't help wondering) realise that this was half the battle?
God inspires the thirst. Out of this experience comes sincere
exploration — and remember, he who seeks will find!

3.   Here is a peep inside an anxious and troubled soul:
tears...tears...tears...Yet at the same time the awful feeling that,
because of his faith in God, this anguish should not be. This

113

sense of inward conflict is being repeated again and again in these later days of Christ-consciousness: "But I am a Christian; I shouldn't feel like this". But you do.

4.   There had been good times when the Psalmist had overflowed with praise and joy. He had been borne up by the throng. He had been uplifted by the exuberance of corporate worship.

5-8.   The writer is baring his soul again. He is both talking to himself and talking to God. This is not an uncommon experience. We do right to ask ourselves questions. This is why keeping a journal of our up and down experiences can be therapeutic. As we look back to it flashes of insight may come.

Now the Psalmist has a flash of insight. It surfaces in what we have come to know as 'the power of positive thinking'. Taking a deliberate decision to lift one's head during times of darkness so as to be in a better position to receive the blessings of the light. This means keeping going with a prayer discipline and sharing in worship when you do not feel like it. Rewards follow but often not immediately.

9-11.   This is a repetition of the experience previously recounted except that there is the added complication of being jeered at by his enemies. They make fun about what they believe to be the utter uselessness of his faith. His answer?. An expression of sheer confidence and hope. Surely progress has been made.

MEDITATION

Are you thirsty and hungry for greater reality in your
Christian life? Then give thanks to God because you are
on your way.

Do you feel lonely in your search? Then is there
someone with whom you could share your experience?

Tears are not to be ashamed of. They bring release.
Darkness is often the prelude to the dawn. Your
sharpened appetite will mean greater ultimate
satisfaction.

Remember your high moments. Re-live one of them now
and re-capture the feelings associated with that
occasion.

Take strength from the faith of others. Your experience is
shared by many.

Try to hold on to valuable experiences by writing about
them or by expressing them in a drawing or painting.

Recall an experience through which you made
discoveries about yourself and God. Realise how
important it is to hold on to such experiences.

Mood swings are universal but the way some
personalities have been shaped makes them more or
less likely to be affected by moods. Don't be envious of
those who seem to live with a constant equanimity of
mood. Sometimes this is contrived and they are
covering up what is really happening within.

**Remember if you can find God in the depths this will
lead you to the heights.**

**The last note of the psalm breathes confidence. Let this
thought be with you throughout the day and especially
last thing at night.**

*(Note: Psalm 43 is a continuation of Psalm 42 and repeats the
same pattern of struggle. Read it through and notice that this Psalm
also ends on an exactly similar note of triumph.)*

SORRY, LORD.   Psalm 51

This Psalm is associated with a particular incident in King David's life: his passion for Bathsheba and his consequent sin in arranging for Uriah, her husband, to be killed in battle, so that he could take her for his wife. This act may seem more serious in our day than in King David's time when people of power and influence regularly did just as they pleased to satisfy their desires. However in this case his deed was courageously challenged by the prophet Nathan *(see 2 Sam. 12:1-15)*.

The Psalm is a genuine cry of sorrow for a particular sin; a realistic acknowledgement of the failure and an earnest appeal for forgiveness, cleansing and renewal. It has become a classic vehicle for the expression of deep sorrow and a longing for a new beginning. Part of its value lies in its specific nature. Our failures may be different but they are just as real.

1-5. Out it all comes in a torrent of words of regret, sorrow and deep longing. The reality of his sin is openly acknowledged and furthermore it is stated to be a sin against God and God only. This cannot mean that it was not a sin against Uriah and Bathsheba! (Some scholars have used this as evidence that the Psalm does not relate to the Bathsheba incident at all.) It is surely a kind of poetic extravagance. David is so concerned about offending God and it is God's forgiveness he desires above all others. It is this ruptured relationship that he wants to put right and in mitigation he tries to put part of the blame on to his forbears. This is a good example of rationalisation and is not unknown in these days of psychological insights. Inadequate parenting should never be used as an excuse for failure. Although it may be a predisposing factor we remain responsible for our own actions.

6-7.   Here we get to the heart of the matter. As Jesus taught sin begins in the heart; in the inward person through jealousy, lust, selfishness, envy (see Mark 7:14-23). It then spreads out into the things we do and the things we refrain from doing. Mature self-awareness brings realities to the surface which have to be dealt with. This self-awareness can come through quiet meditation, sharing with another, counselling, sacramental confession, or a combination of several of these factors. But a word of caution — we must not become morbid and go searching for sins that do not exist. Nor should we equate normal sexual desire with sin. It is what we do about our various desires which matters — as David discovered to his cost.

8-12.   These sublime poetic sentences express a deep longing for the cleansing process to take place and for there to be positive renewal in the depths of his heart, mind and soul. He is in the gutter, filthy and unable to stand (bones broken). He longs to be fit to be in the presence of the Lord — "ransomed, healed, restored, forgiven".

13-19.   Now the sinner has been cleansed he can return to God. He can also take others with him in the same condition. Furthermore he can now praise God and share in worship. His burden has been lifted and not because an animal sacrifice has been made, but because there has been sorrow and deep repentance. This is what is pleasing to God.

MEDITATION

Are we specific enough about our own failures when we come to God, say in the Communion Service?

Do we attempt to make excuses — to rationalise?

God's forgiveness often depends upon our making reparation and actively seeking reconciliation with those we have wronged.

Forgiveness and healing go together. To feel forgiven is to experience a sense of release which, in turn, triggers healthy energies.

Do we all recognise that we each have a dark side to our personalities?

What disciplines do we practice to enable us to discern the realities within?

Remember — God is not against us — He is for us.

Visualise a dirty floor surface being cleaned until it shines and is alive with freshness. Then see a similar process taking place within yourself. Quietly rejoice.

God does not ban sinners from His presence. We ban ourselves. Once we go to Him with our sin and are sincerely penitent, then cleansing takes place.

Worship which follows on from forgiveness is joyful and full of meaning. Note the way the Communion Service is constructed. The Gloria comes after the act of confession and the declaration of forgiveness.

The final offerings we bring will not be excuses for our failure but a spontaneous outburst of praise.

DYNAMIC WORSHIP   Psalm 84

This Psalm has one dominant theme — Praise! If another
person helps you out of a very difficult and dangerous situation
you instinctively want to thank them, and probably convey your
thanks in a practical way by means of a gift. The regular
worship in which many of us participate is not always easily
connected with an acute sense of deliverance. For this reason
our worship requires thought and preparation. One of the
problems with the Praise aspect of worship is that the medium
used becomes more important than what is going on inside the
mind and heart of the worshipper. The catchy tunes we use in
our Prayer and Praise meetings. The sonorous beauty of Choral
Evensong. We can so easily be captivated by the vehicle we are
using that true praise and thanksgiving does not rise up from
the heart. I remember being frowned on once when attending
Choral Eucharist in a Cathedral because I was singing the
Psalms. The implication was that I was not there to participate
but to be a passive observer! This Psalm suggests the kind of
experiences which give rise to real thankfulness which is then
expressed in true worship.

The Psalm divides into three natural sections with three
different groups represented in each section: the professionals,
the pilgrims and the interested onlookers.

1-4.   These felicitous words express the enormous sense of
privilege felt by those who actually live in 'the courts of the
Lord'. They came to appreciate its beauty and splendour just as
the occupants of a Cathedral Close come to love the soaring
spires and majestic towers of their Cathedral. To both such the
sanctuary becomes home, so much so that even the birds have
a place (even the pigeons!!). There is a strong mystical feeling

about these experiences and perhaps a little poetic exaggeration in the expressions used. But the reality breaks through — it is a humbling but uplifting experience to be called upon to celebrate on behalf of others.

5-8.   In this section the worshipper is a pilgrim who has come up to the Temple for the Harvest Thanksgiving. For many it was a long journey but the ways travelled had not just been physical; they were also spiritual and within the heart. As they passed through a dry and unlovely valley they had experienced rain and this had meant a transformation. Where previously there had been barreness, life had sprang forth. What goodness! What grace! And there happening before their eyes. Thus the two roads they were travelling, the physical and the spiritual were connected and within themselves the dry places were blossoming and producing fruits. Here were the roots of authentic worship — within experience. Thus into the mould provided by the professionals they poured these living discoveries and thus they truly worshipped.

9-12.   Now we get the view of the wistful onlooker. In all probability he was a soldier who stood guard on the temple. He was not there to worship but to do a job. Yet it soon dawned on him that just to be there was a privilege — even as a doorkeeper. He also had something to offer. He lifts up his shield as an act of devotion and the face of his shield reflects the glory of the Lord. Finally the professionals, the pilgrims and interested observers, are all gathered into a glorious act of thanksgiving, the heart and centre of which is trust in the living God.

MEDITATION

Think about the dangers and temptations which surround our religious professionals — familiarity — the role taking over from the person.

What can we do to enable our ministers and priests to remain fully human? How can we safeguard their health and facilitate their healing?

Can the sanctuary sometimes become a hiding place for all of us?

William Temple once said that the world would be saved by worship. How?

During the week do we make a note of those things we will especially give thanks for in Sunday worship?

How marvellous when infectious faith makes a difference to life in the sour and bitter places. Use your imagination and see the dry, barren valleys being transformed. Then let the same things happen within yourself.

Praise is an essential part of the balanced life. It creates generosity. Do we need to cultivate the art of thanksgiving? Practise it now.

What helps casual observers to become dedicated participants?

Those who truly worship can never treat other people as 'things'.

Pray for the professionals. Pray for reality in your pilgrim worship. Pray that living worship will attract the interested onlookers...

WONDER, LOVE AND PRAISE   Psalm 139: 1-18 and 23-24

I am offering this meditation in a format different from the others. By itself, without any comments, this Psalm provides material for a full-scale devotional exercise which includes healthy self-examination. So, first of all we will read it through slowly, letting each sentence and phrase reach home. I have omitted verses 19-22 because they break the sequence of thought and reveal a totally different side of the Psalmist's mind. This is more evidence of the essential reality of the Psalms and their dealing with every aspect of human feeling, including the desire for revenge.

So I have taken a phrase which I believe summarises each section and reflected upon it. Then I have selected a poem or relevant quotation to further illustrate the theme. After the initial reading through, we shall come back to each section in turn and let the title words be the key to opening the treasure, reinforced by the poem, or quotation.

1-6 SEARCH AND KNOW

We often talk about our own search for God. The other side of the coin is God's search for us. In Christian terms we call this grace, which is God's love in action directed towards us (see 1 John 4:19).

The other aspect of God's search for us is his discerning of our true natures, which includes our motivation or, as we sometimes say, "what makes us tick".

Remember that there are two kinds of knowledge. There is factual knowledge which is often related to special interests or intellectual pursuits, and there is the knowledge of awareness which relates to our intuition and to our feelings. Spiritual insights often come via this channel and they should be treasured.

Looking at things from another point of view, Julian of Norwich said:

> We ought to have three kinds of knowledge. The first is that we know our Lord God. The second is that we know ourselves, what we are through him in nature and in grace. The third is that we know humbly that our self is opposed to sin and weakness.

Julian's life was in itself a quest for spiritual reality but as a result she was able to say:

> Our good Lord answered to all the questions and doubts I could raise, saying most comfortably: "I may make all things well and I can make all things well, and I shall make all things well and I will make all things well; and you will see for yourself that every kind of thing will be well."

7-12 NO HIDING PLACE

There is no escape from God in the end. Every possible pathway is explored. In the beginning there is God and at the end there will still be God. But do we need a hiding place if we want to be in his presence? Why not simply dwell on God's sufficiency and be grateful.

There is also another comforting thought — or is it a
disturbing one? We may turn our backs upon him and try to
forget him. He will never forget us, nor turn away from us.

> Love must express and communicate itself.
> That's its nature.
> When people begin to love one another,
> they start telling everything that's happened to them,
> every detail of their daily life.
> They 'reveal' themselves to each other,
> unbosom themselves and exchange confidences.
>
> God hasn't ceased being Revelation
> any more than He's ceased being Love.
> He enjoys expressing Himself,
> sharing His secrets,
> communicating with us
> and revealing Himself to anyone
> who wants to listen.

(Louis Evely)

13-18 ALL SYSTEMS GO

What makes a human being? Perhaps the better question is
who? We know a lot about physical development. We know a
great deal now about psychological development. But what
power is it which holds every aspect of being together in such
ways as to make it possible for us to be the worst of sinners or
the greatest of saints?

These marvellous possibilities arise out of God's mind. What
we are in our totality is due to God's creative actions.
Everything that is, originated in his mind.

Surely this stimulates thought about the sheer privilege of life
and the stewardship of body, mind and spirit which is ours. We
are 'fearfully and wonderfully made' Are we co-operating with
God for that bit of his creation for which we, under him, are
responsible?

One day people will touch and talk perhaps easily,
And loving be as natural as breathing and warm as
sunlight,
And people will untie themselves,
as string is unknotted,
Unfold and yawn and stretch and spread
their fingers,
Unfurl, uncurl, like seaweed returning to the sea.
And work will be simple and swift,
as a seagull flying,
and play will be casual and quiet,
as a seagull settling.
And the clocks will stop, and no one will wonder
or care, or notice,
And people will smile without reason,
even in the rain.

A.S.J. Tessimond

Christ came that I might really be me... that I might
grow into maturity... by nothing less than the fulness of
the stature of Christ himself.

Brother Bernard SF

126

Section 5

SEVEN
GENERAL
MEDITATIONS

SINGING THE CREATOR'S SONG

(Begin with the organ — or some other instrument — playing quietly the hymn tune Deep Harmony)

To be healthy is to be in tune with the song the Creator is eternally singing *(Canon Sidney Evans).*

God's tune for your life is unique. It is yours and yours alone. Each of us is given the task of discovering what that tune is; then to endeavour to read and interpret the music. Finally, to play it on the instrument of our lives.

How may you be enabled to sing the Creator's song?

1.   BY BEING IN TUNE WITH GOD

Remember, God is a person, not an abstract force — and God loves you as though you were the only other person in the world.

Remember, God is on your side. He is ceaselessly working on your behalf. He is not against you.

The Christian Faith is not primarily about rules and regulations; it is based on grace which is God's love in action directed towards you.

Wholeness is not about perfection; it is about the growing maturity which comes from growing self-awareness and developing God-awareness.

You are accepted — just as you are — warts and all. The only adequate response is GRATITUDE.

2. BY BEING IN TUNE WITH OURSELVES

I am large. I contain a multitude *(Walt Whitman)*.

The good which I want to do, I fail to do; but what I do is the wrong which is against my will *(Romans 7:19)*.

First acknowledge your internal divisions. They will always be with you but hopefully, because of grace, they will become less and less.

Recognise that there is always a residual 'child' within you leading you into 'childish' ways.

Ask God to put his finger upon one aspect of your 'childishness' — now!

Might sharing ourselves with a trusted friend or spiritual adviser be of help?

When did I last laugh at myself?

Remember, God's will for you is wholeness. The Bible invites you to enjoy the Shalom experience — harmony — integration — togetherness.

Ask God for this gift — now! Even a small experience of Shalom will lead on to greater expectations — and bigger consequences.

3. BY BEING IN TUNE WITH OTHER PEOPLE

Life is made up of a network of relationships.

Think of three people you don't like — why don't you like them?

Think of three people you do like — why do you like them?

We tend to dislike people whose personalities are similar to our own.

We tend to like people who affirm us, appreciate us and encourage us.

Does this tell us anything about how we might try to change our attitudes towards people we do not instinctively like?

When we try to see people 'in Christ' we often become more aware of the burdens they carry and the limitations they have to live with.

Being more vulnerable ourselves with others often breaks down barriers.

Is compassion an art to be practised?

CONCLUSION

> Glad Amen...
> When the chorus of 'I am's
> Surrenders to the solo —
> HE IS!

That solo is the Creator's song — and he invites us to both play and sing it with and through the one instrument we really possess — that of our lives.

(This meditation could well be used with a background of soft Taizé chanting and periods of silence in between the sentences.)

THE HEALING POWER OF FORGIVENESS

Dr. Loring T. Swain was a physician who lectured in arthritic diseases at Harvard Medical School. In addition to treating his patients with the latest medical and physical therapies, he also prescribed a spiritual therapy for those who were receptive and willing.

The basis upon which his spiritual therapy was founded was that feelings and emotions like RESENTMENT — BITTERNESS — REVENGE — JEALOUSY — UNFORGIVENESS — affect the body chemistry and this, in turn, can cause some forms of arthritic disorders and peptic and duodenal ulcers. An important aspect of treatment is therefore to encourage more positive ways of thinking so that these negative feelings and emotions can be countered and overcome.

These more positive possibilities are now brought before us first to think about and reflect upon, then to express through prayer our desire for grace and for resources to strengthen our inner being.

1. BE LOVING

You must love the Lord your God... You must love your fellow-man/woman as you love yourself.

(Matthew 22:37-39)

We have been given one another to love and be loved and to learn again on a deeper level that giving is taking and all is grace.

(Werner Pelz)

No person is whole who is not joined to the sufferings of
others.

(R.A. Lambourne)

A PRAYER

> Jesus, the first and last,
> On thee my soul is cast;
> Thou didst thy work begin,
> By blotting out my sin,
> Thou wilt the root remove,
> And perfect me in love.

(Charles Wesley)

2. APOLOGISE GRACEFULLY

So if you are to offer your gift to God at the altar and there
you remember that your brother has something against you,
leave your gift there in front of the altar and go at once and
make peace with your brother; then come back and offer your
gift to God.

(Matthew 5:23-24)

A proper and meaningful apology releases something vital
within one's self and often does the same within the heart of
the other person concerned. Thus apology (which may include
confession) paves the way for mutual forgiveness and
reconciliation.

A PRAYER

Lord, we now think by name of any to whom we feel we
should go with words of sorrow and regret:

Give us the courage to be open and honest with them and to
speak what we believe to be the truth in love. Lord, we seek a
positive response but prepare our hearts and minds for
whatever may be the outcome of our initiative.

And now we pray for them by name and we pray for ourselves.
May there be the fruits of repentance on all sides and also the
joy of reconciliation.

Amen.

3. FORGIVE GENEROUSLY

Do not judge others so that God will not judge you.

Do for others what you want them to do for you.
(Matthew 7:1 and 12)

The underlying choice for all is whether we are going God's
way, co-operating, yielding to him... or whether we choose
independence in a world of our own constructing... Getting
ourselves right with God opens the way for discovering the
inner harmony and congruence and unity of all that is, and the
significance of each part of it.

(Brother Bernard, SF)

When you forgive generously you sometimes set a chain re-
action going. A father who forgives his daughter's murderers
sends a light shining right across the world. Jesus, the one who
forgave, is remembered with gratitude and honoured. His noble
example is frequently forgotten — and the whole world is the
poorer because of it.

A PRAYER

"Forgive our sins, as we forgive".
You taught us, Lord, to pray;
But you alone can grant us grace
To live the words we say.

How can your pardon reach and bless
The unforgiving heart
That broods on wrong; and will not let
Old bitterness depart?

Lord, cleanse the depths within our souls,
And bid resentment cease;
Then, reconciled to God and man,
Our lives will spread your peace.

(Rosamund E. Herklots)

4. CHANGE WILLINGLY

Take the log out of your own eye first, and then you will be
able to see to take out the speck from your brother's eye.

(Matthew 7.5)

Radical, fundamental change is difficult to achieve in one's
personal life. Character and personality patterns are laid down
at a very early age and it is not as easy to change as some
people seem to suppose. Adjustment is however change. We
may be nervous and timid because of lack of security in
childhood but if the reality can be faced and acknowledged, the
fears may not entirely depart but they can be overcome.

At the deepest part of all of us there is that which can only be
itself when it lets go beyond itself. So, in relation to God, we

become ourselves. He does not destroy what he has made but
gently enables it to be itself. This union of our spirit with his,
or rather his with ours, is life itself. Letting go into this reality
relieves us, renews us, reinvigorates us, excites us, equips us
with energy for whatever the task.

(Brother Bernard, SF)

A PRAYER

Make me a captive, Lord,
And then I shall be free;
Force me to render up my sword,
And I shall conqueror be.
I sink in life's alarms
When by myself I stand;
Imprison me within thine arms,
And strong shall be my hand.

My will is not my own
Till thou hast made it thine;
If it would reach a monarch's throne
It must its crown resign.
It only stands unbent,
Amid the clashing strife,
When on thy bosom it has leant
And found in thee its life.

(George Matheson)

Finally go through each section again and end by saying
together:

**LORD ENABLE US TO BE LOVING; TO APOLOGISE
GRACEFULLY, TO FORGIVE GENEROUSLY AND TO
CHANGE WILLINGLY.**

AMEN.

A JOURNEY THROUGH LIFE

Go back to your childhood days and think about your parents.
Whether still alive or not greet them each in turn. Allow your
feelings to flow naturally towards them, whatever those feelings
are. Do you feel a need to put things right between you — then
do so. This may include you offering them your forgiveness or
you seeking theirs — or both. If they are still alive then some
practical consequences may follow. If not, you need the mental
and emotional release that may well come from this
engagement.

Try to re-live some of the key moments of your childhood:

    a) Times when you felt loved, happy and secure.
    b) Times when you felt unloved, unhappy and insecure.

Give thanks for the feelings of emotional warmth you have been
able to recapture. Ask for God's warmth for the cold parts
which remain.

> What is soiled, make thou pure,
> What is wounded, work its cure;
> What is parched, fructify;
> What is rigid, gently bend;
> What is frozen, warmly tend;
> Straighten what goes erringly.

(Veni Sanctus Spiritus)

Think of your teenage years and the excitement of your
growing and developing sexuality. Acknowledge, if it was so,
your feelings that your sexuality was sinful. Express, if valid,
your thankfulness on discovering your mistake and rejoice in
your sexuality as a vital part of God's creation.

Reflect on the challenges of your teenage years and bring to
mind the people who helped you and influenced you for good.
Thank them and thank God. Forgive any whom you feel
wronged you or harmed you.

> A bruised reed he will not break,
> and a dimly burning wick he will not quench.
>
> The place of failure is the place God finds us
> with his grace.
>
> Prayer is a relationship with God in which failure
> is tasted very bitterly, suffered with love and
> allowed to become the place of resurrection.

Think of your present situation. What are you anxious about?
(Make a list.) What are you sorry for? (Tell God and seek
forgiveness.) Describe those things you feel truly thankful for.
(Praise God!) Check on your progress. Do you feel nearer to
God or further away from him than at some earlier stages of
your life? Have you someone with whom you feel you could
share your deepest needs? Should you be doing something
about it? Do you tend to hide behind a mask of professionalism
or respectability?

> Grace is that moment when we see in ourselves
> what we had not seen before.
> The whole Jesus demands the whole person.
>
> O Lord my God, I cry to you from the place
> where I am at present. Please make me whole.

THE SPACE BETWEEN

In the space between us
is the hope for our healing.
Quiet
Compassionate
Space.
To be filled,
not with activity,
but still presence.
To be bridged
not with demand,
but affirmation.
Space
in which to move
to the music of love,
to reach gently
for the touch
of intimate understanding.

But space too
for the naming of pain,
the owning
of anger,
the touching
of terror.
Space to bring
nightmares into the light,
to find the shards
of shattered dreams.

So let there be space between us.
Growing space.
Breathing space.
Healing space.
Do not crush me with your kindness,
Nor yet permit me to possess your pain.

Let there be space
for God to breathe in.

(Veronica Faulks)

COMPLEMENTARY GOSPEL VALUES

Vital truth will come to us now as we reflect upon a short series of what may seem to be at first, opposing values. Yet, as we shall see, they are actually complementary. Out of our own internal dialogue may come new insights and thus progress in the Christian life.

1. SELF-ESTEEM AND SELF-DENIAL

You matter to God: "Fear not, for I have redeemed you; I have called you by your name, you are mine." God does not make junk.

Only from a proper basis of self-worth can come realistic self-denial. The discipline of self-denial requires the mature base of self-esteem.

Give yourself value but remember that we follow one who said: "Take up your cross and follow me".

2. MINISTRY AND LEISURE

Ministry, both lay and ordained, is a continuation of the work of Christ for the sake of the Kingdom.

To stay effective, outgoing ministry needs to be balanced by interesting and stimulating leisure pursuits.

Ministry is often demanding and intensive; thus it requires the release that is derived from wholesome leisure.

"If you don't stop to admire the daisies, you'll soon be pushing them up."

3. FRIENDSHIP AND GENERATIVITY

The spiritual journey requires deep and abiding friendships. We all need to discover how to receive gracefully and to give generously.

Generativity means fruitfulness. We can bear fruit among our friends, but we can also 'generate', produce fruit in the lives of those with whom we find friendship difficult.

4. PRAYER AND HUMOUR

Prayer reveals a hunger and a yearning for God and further spiritual enlightenment.

Holiness is the capacity to laugh and to play as well as pray.

By placing us in the presence of God, prayer provides us with a vantage point from which we can see the world from another perspective; the perspective of the coming reign of God. This allow us to relax and laugh.

5. COMMUNITY AND SOLITUDE

The love that makes us whole usually begins with the love of our families — but sadly this is not always true.

There is no such thing as a Christian existence that is not part of an effective network of people who share one Lord, one Faith and one Baptism. We live and learn and thus grow and develop within our respective Christian Communities.

But community must always make room for solitude. Solitude is time spent alone for the purpose of encountering ourselves

and the living God. Without a foundation in solitude a spiritual
life is like a house built on sand — shallowly grounded and
easily eroded.

A PRAYER

**Lord, make us whole. Blend together all those different
aspects of our being so that body, mind, spirit and emotions
are so integrated as to make us real persons; acceptable to
ourselves and to you; ready to be useful in your service.**

AMEN.

*(The headings for this Meditation were provided by Wilkie Au, SJ,
in his book* By Way of the Heart.*)*

LIVING IS LOVING

Love is letting go. surrendering, becoming one,
Love is openness, commitment,
To love is to make yourself vulnerable,
an interplay of pain and joy,
of poverty and riches.

Grant us this grace we beseech you, O Lord.

Love is being available,
helping, rendering a service,
shielding the other from disappointment.

Grant us this grace we beseech you, O Lord.

To love is to create space,
where the other can be himself/herself,
It is enabling all his/her finest qualities to flower.
Love is communication, partnership, exchange.

Grant us this grace we beseech you, O Lord.

To love is to encourage, to value,
to give strength,
to accept the other as he/she is,
with his/her weaknesses and strengths.

Grant us this grace we beseech you, O Lord.

Love is not judging by what one sees,
by achievements, successes and results.
Love is not asking:
"What can you give me?"
but, "What can I give you?"

Grant us this grace we beseech you, O Lord.

Love is warmth and life,
goodness and sorrow,
happiness and pain.
Love is unfathomable,
inexhaustible,
a mystery.
To love is to become the other.

Write all these words on our hearts we beseech you, O Lord.

Love, rich in a poor stable,
Love, discounted on a cross;
Glorious in resurrection,
Tangible in human lives,
made beautiful today.

**Lord, help me to reach out and touch it... today...
tomorrow... and in eternity.**

*(This is a Grail Meditation by J. de Rooy and is taken from the
booklet* Tools for Meditation. *It is used by permission.)*

WHOLENESS IS GOD'S GIFT

Introduction to Meditation

How do we become whole persons? Perhaps we shouldn't try.
Certainly it has nothing to do with struggling to be perfect, in
spite of what Jesus said to his disciples in Matthew 5:48. A
study of the word translated 'perfect' in the New Testament
suggests a relationship with the Old Testament word 'Shalom'
which means completeness, total integrity, inward harmony.
Building on this the New Testament adds the concept of
maturity; the ability to live an integrated life. Perfection has
somehow come to mean living every detail of life without fault
or error. Those who strive after this ideal seek to screw up
their energies to reach some unattainable ideal. It just does not
work and those who try often become casualties of their own
making.

Those I know who seem to be as near to being whole persons
as I can comprehend are not intense people; rather they are
'laid back'. at ease with themselves; able to share themselves
with others and to communicate well. They admit to there
being 'dark corners' in their lives but these they accept. They
know, in their wisdom, that God hasn't finished with them yet.

In this meditation you are invited to listen to God as he quietly
reassures you; as he makes his and your position quite clear.
The pattern will be to use simple words and sentences,
including some quotations to help you to do your own business
with God. Sometimes you will hear soft music in the
background. Don't concentrate on that. Just enjoy it as it rolls
over you and you make your own response to the various
affirmations and suggestions.

THE MEDITATION

Stage 1.   ACCEPT GOD'S LOVE

Here are words you can trust:

> You are precious in my sight and honoured —
> and I love you.
>
> *(Isaiah 43:4)*

> In this is love, not that we loved God,
> but that he loved us.
>
> *(1 John 4:10)*

So how do we accept this love? How do we make it our own?
Simply by thanking God and saying, "Lord, I accept your love
for me as being sufficient for my needs". This is the only
beginning possible on the pilgrim path towards wholeness. You
have really known this from the very start. Now just allow the
warm air of God's love to enfold you. Be quiet and rest in him.

> Loved with everlasting love,
> Led by grace that love to know;
> Spirit, breathing from above,
> Thou hast taught me it is so.
>
> *(George Wade Robinson)*

Say quietly to yourself: God accepts me just as I am... God
loves me in spite of what I am...

(Quiet music)

Stage 2. BE LOVING

Remember the assurance given to us in Stage 1 that God took the initiative in loving us. Now hear about the required consequences of that divine activity:

> *We love* because God first loved us.
>
> *(1 John 4:19)*

Here are some further words to guide you:

> To love is not to give of your riches,
> but to reveal to others their riches,
> their gifts, their value, and to trust them
> and their capacity to grow.
>
> *(Jean Vanier)*

> We have been placed in our togetherness
> in order to be seen to be our brother's and sister's
> keepers. This togetherness is God's grace.
>
> *(Werner Pelz)*

> Love is not doing the extraordinary,
> but doing the ordinary things in life
> competently and well.
>
> *(Kahlil Gibran)*

> The beginning of love for the brethren
> is learning to listen to them.
>
> *(Dietrich Bonhoeffer)*

Beloved let us love,
for the loving
is the sending
and the mending
and the end
of the strife-hate
in the heart of man
Christ love
Abba.

(Source Unknown)

(Quiet music)

Stage 3.   CONTINUE IN PRAYER

It is this discipline which makes it all possible. Not that it is
all that simple nor will it necessarily be easy going all the way.
That master of the inner life, Thomas Merton, had his message
to the world summed up for him in this way:

> I don't have all the answers. Live the questions. There is
> struggle. Be free. Be yourself. How? By prayer. By prayer
> I don't mean always saying prayers. I mean that kind of
> prayer in which you leave your phoney self behind and
> find your true self in God. At the same time we find
> everybody else there. And we realise that we are all one
> in God and everything else follows.
> *(Basil Pennington)*

In prayer we are called to find and love God in the
concrete experiences of our lives. As with Moses before
the burning bush, the place where we stand is holy
ground. So we are called to take our experiences to prayer
and to recognise the risen Christ in faces and features not
his own.

(Wilkie Au SJ)

150

So let life flow into prayer and let prayer flow into life. Herein lies the secret. There can be no separation of life into the sacred and the secular. All life is God's and he is available in all life's varied experiences.

(Quiet music)

So now let us go back through the three stages:

1. YOU ARE LOVED

2. BE LOVING

3. CONTINUE IN PRAYER

There is only one truly whole person. His name is Jesus. And he will accompany us on our pilgrimage *towards wholeness*.

Section 6

SEVEN SUGGESTIONS
FOR
HEALTH AND HEALING SERVICES

A HEALING SERVICE BASED ON THE MEDITATION ON LOVE (pages 145/146)

Introduction:

The famous Welsh Rugby International, Cliff Morgan, was asked in a television interview about his outstanding childhood memory. His reply was, "Being part of a loving family and belonging to a loving and caring community".

This meditation suggests that:

1. LOVE IS MOVING OUT

Parents of teenagers often hear this cry from their children: "The trouble is you don't understand. The world is different from when you were our age. Life has moved on."

Hard though it is to accept there is truth in this plea. We do need to 'move out' and to try to understand the difference in culture patterns between our youthful years and theirs.

Think of the people who have really helped you in your life. Did they 'move out' in understanding sympathy and try to understand your position and to empathise with it?

Do we need to 'move out' to create better understanding between races, religions, Christian denominations?

Just reflect upon the healing implications of 'moving out'.

154

2. LOVE IS AVAILABILITY — CREATING SPACE

People get 'all mixed up' at various stages in life — not only in
the teenage years. When they do they need someone to make
themselves available, to 'create space' for them to use.
Availability is not only a matter of time; it is allowing people in
need to become aware of our real selves. Honest vulnerability
will sometimes trigger off deep confession and real sharing.

The phrase 'a wounded healer' is becoming commonplace —
but it conveys a vital truth. As our wounds have become part
of our personalities so they can be used to bring healing to
others.

3. LOVE IS ENCOURAGEMENT

To feel valued, appreciated, affirmed, encouraged, is a necessity
for all human beings. The author of our Meditation links
acceptance with encouragement. The two do go together.
Some people it is easy to accept and encourage. Others prove
difficult but perhaps they are in the greatest need.

You do not necessarily have to agree with all the people you try
to encourage. Part of the process of encouragement may be to
listen to their point of view.

Love as encouragement is a form of preventive health care. It
helps people to be more real; to draw upon their own resources
because they recognise themselves as being of worth. Oil the
wheels of life by practising encouragement for others — every
day. Such actions have healing consequences.

4. LOVE IS WARMTH

Genuine warmth is demonstrated by our attitudes towards
people. Warmth is related to genuineness. Most of us strive
to play parts; we wear masks — thus we are not real in our
dealing with others.

If we opt out of difficult circumstances and relationships
because we fear the consequences we minimise ourselves. As we
take risks and get involved in life and with people — we create
warmth. And as a practical result other people's lives improve.
They become part of God's drive towards personal and social
wholeness.

> Life is meant for loving, Lord if this be true,
> Love of life and neighbour, springs from love of you.
> Give us your compassion; yours the name we bear;
> Yours the only victory we would serve and share.

(F. Pratt Green)

A HEALING SERVICE BASED ON THE OLD TESTAMENT WORD 'SHALOM'

The Old Testament word 'Shalom' means much more than 'peace' which is its usual translation. It can be said to mean, TOGETHERNESS, HARMONY, BALANCE, INTEGRATION, WHOLENESS.

Try and answer the following four sets of questions in the quietness of your own heart. After you have done this within the atmosphere of this act of worship, take the questionnaire home and use it in your private devotions.

1. SHALOM PEOPLE ARE SEEKING TO RELATE TO GOD

Do you find that personal prayer...

    a)   comes naturally?

    b)   is a struggle to maintain?

    c)   is so difficult that you have given up?

In the past twelve months have you...

    a)   made progress in your relationship with God?

    b)   made any new discoveries which have enriched your discipleship?

    c)   carried on the same old tread-mill?

2. SHALOM PEOPLE ARE TRYING TO FIND THEMSELVES

Do you find talking about your needs to another person...

- a) so embarassasing that you don't?
- b) not necessary?
- c) difficult but you have made the effort?

Do you wear a mask to hide your real feelings because...

- a) you want to be liked?
- b) you want to maintain your 'glittering image'?
- c) you feel it right to do so anyway?

3. SHALOM PEOPLE BELONG TO A COMMUNITY OF UNDERSTANDING

Do you feel that within your Church Fellowship...

- a) you are loved?
- b) people appreciate your worth?
- c) you need people to be more outgoing towards you?

Do you think that your Church is organised...

- a) to care for people adequately?
- b) to meet people's deep needs when they arrive?
- c) to enable people of different views to hold together in love?

4. SHALOM PEOPLE ACT RESPONSIBLY TOWARDS GOD'S CREATED UNIVERSE

Do you feel that environmental and 'green' issues...

    a) are matters which relate to discipleship?
    b) should be left to the politicians?
    c) call for you to be involved?

How are you involved in...

    a) healthy eating and gardening?
    b) organic gardening?
    c) political 'green' issues?

A SERVICE ON PREVENTIVE HEALTH CARE

We are all concerned about our health. When we are ill we want, more than anything else, to get well and take up our normal activities again. Our hearts go out to people whose lives are restricted by crippling illness.

Many years ago Dr. Leslie Weatherhead wrote a small book entitled *10 Minutes a Day — For Health's Sake*. It was of course about prayer. A London vicar has more people attending his church for mid-week relaxation sessions than at Sunday worship. City business men are helped to discover quiet within themselves and to relax physically with the help of simple guided exercises. A London heart specialist, Dr Peter Nixon, has invited patients to spend two weeks with a community of nuns in the hope that this will bring about a change in their frantic, high-pressured life style. They also are helped to find quiet within themselves and to relax.

Here is what one beneficiary has written:

> "It has contributed to many changes in my life. Not only has it made me more relaxed, physically and mentally, but also it has contributed to changes in my personality and my way of life. I seem to have become calmer, more open and receptive, especially to ideas which have been unknown to me or very different from my past way of life. I like the way I am becoming more patient, overcoming some fears especially around my physical health and stamina. I feel stronger physically and mentally. I take better care of myself. I am a more committed person".

Of course true Christian prayer is much more than a device to
secure better health. It must never be used only as a means to
that kind of end. But if better health is a by-product of
meaningful prayer then this is surely God's plan. Perhaps we
have over-spiritualised our faith and paid insufficient attention
to our bodies. Salvation is about the renewal of the whole
person. To be 'saved' is to be 'healthy' in body, mind and
spirit.

The congregation is then invited to hear — and to follow in
their pew Bibles — John Chapter 15:1-17, The True Vine.

Thoughts are then extracted from the passage as a basis for
meditation.

STRIP DOWN

Useless baggage is to be got rid of. This means self-discipline.
The tool for 'stripping down' is 'the message' (verse 3). As we
are open to the gospel we feel that certain aspects of our lives
are not in conformity with His will. So we seek to be rid of
them. Not easy but necessary.

ABIDE IN HIM

Would-be slimmers are told to "think thin". Disciples are
invited to "think Jesus" — to "hide his word in our hearts".
To think of Jesus and all that he stands for first thing in the
morning and last thing at night. Then he will come into our
minds at other times as well.

Four words to help us:

LOOK to Jesus... LEAN on Jesus... LONG for Jesus... LOVE
Jesus and be assured that you are loved by him.

161

"I take hold of the branch,
it feels strong and supple.
I rest my whole weight upon it.
The branch holds.

But here on the ground,
beneath my feet — another branch.
I pick it up. It snaps sharply and lies
broken in my hand.

Why should one be strong and full of life —
and the other ready for the fire?

The reason is plain:
The one is held and life flows from the roots,
through the trunk, to the branches.

The other is dead because it has become
separated from the trunk.

How do I remain alive with his life?

'This is my body, broken for you.'

'This is my blood, shed for you.'

These glorious gifts you offer me —
that your life might be in me and that
my life might be full.

So am I 'held'.

So shall I live!"

(From *Stepping-Stones to Christian Maturity* by Howard
Booth. Published by Arthur James Ltd)

A SERVICE OF ANOINTING

Anointing was a regular practice in the Early Church, used together with prayer for the sick. It was also used in baptism and confirmation, and, later, in the ordination of ministers and the coronation of monarchs. Within the Roman Church, anointing developed into a last rite for the dying. For many years anointing as a sacrament of healing died out. It is a ministry slowly being recovered by the Church.

As with the ministry of the laying on of hands, it is important to understand that anointing for healing means more than just a seeking for physical cure; that it is more closely related to love and prayer than to magic; that the oil is not about sickness but about life and health; that the ministry is not ours but God's and the healing is not ours but Christ's through the working of the Holy Spirit. Anointing is not administered because all else has failed but as part of the continuing ministry of God in Christ — a ministry being shared with many others — doctors, nurses, family and friends — a part which is the particular concern of a praying and believing church.

The oil is a sign of the renewing power of God and of his will that we should all be reconciled to him and made whole in Jesus Christ. The anointing indicates the giving of the entire situation into the hands of God who knows all our needs. For this reason anointing is usually administered once only in a particular illness.

The order of service for anointing may be part of a service for the laying on of hands or it can be used separately. Much will depend upon the context in which it is being used. It would normally include the reading of scripture (cf James 5:13 ff.), and then prayer for the administration, confession of sin and assurance of pardon as follows:

PRAYER FOR THE ADMINISTRATION OF THE OIL

Almighty God, our Father, graciously grant that by the operation of your Holy Spirit, this oil may be used for the healing of all infirmities. To those who receive it and put their trust in your mercy, may this anointing bring a healing of body, mind and spirit, to the glory of your name. Amen.

PRAYER OF CONFESSION

Have mercy upon us, O God
according to your steadfast love;
according to your abundant mercy,
blot out our transgressions.
Wash us thoroughly from our iniquity,
and cleanse us from our sins.
Create in us a clean heart, O God,
and put a new and right spirit within us.
Cast us not away from your presence,
and take not your Holy Spirit from us.
Restore to us the joy of your salvation,
and uphold us with a willing spirit.

ASSURANCE OF PARDON

If we confess our sins, God is faithful and just, and will forgive our sins, and cleanse us from all unrighteousness.

Take comfort then in the assurance that even those things that are hidden from memory, or are too deep for words, are not beyond God's forgiving love.

May God, who knows us completely, bless you with pardon and peace. Amen.

THE ANOINTING

(The minister dips his thumb in the oil, and makes the sign of the cross on the person's forehead — sometimes also on the open palms — saying...)

> (N...) in the name of the Lord Jesus Christ I anoint you with this sacramental oil that you may receive the anointing of the Holy Spirit, for the healing of all your infirmities, whether of body, mind or spirit. May you be set free from all that troubles you, that you may serve and give thanks to God.

(The laying on of hands may follow, with appropriate prayers. Others may be invited to participate in this act.)

PRAYER OF THANKSGIVING

We give praise and thanks to you, O God. In Jesus Christ, you have given us life, brought healing and forgiveness, quickened our faith and renewed our hope. Keep us ever mindful of your love and mercy, that we may remain your faithful servants all our days. In the name of Jesus Christ. Amen.

BLESSING

David Dale

A HEALTH AND HEALING SERVICE TO BE HELD IN CONNECTION WITH A HEALTH FAIR OR FESTIVAL OF HEALTH

In two inner city churches in recent time I have been made aware of the possibilities of bringing as many of the caring and health agencies as possible together for an exhibition to which the general public is invited. The exhibition consists of displays from both statutory and voluntary agencies with their representatives being present at different times for information and advice.

The following is a list of the organisations which have become involved:
Red Cross
St. John's Ambulance Brigade
Local Health Centre
Counselling Agencies
Relate
Chiropody Service
Dietitians
Audiologist
Optician
Victim Support
Community Police
Mind (mental health)
Age Concern
Law Centre including welfare rights
Leisure Centre
General Practitioners
Community Nurses
Health Visitors
Dentists

Complementary Therapists
Drugs Team
Well Men (including Stop Smoking)
Well Women
Meals on Wheels
Community Hospital
Local Hospice
Social Services
NSPCC

The climax of such a Festival should be a well planned act of worship preferably arranged on an ecumenical basis. The initiative might even come from a local Council of Churches. Representatives from all participating organisations would be invited, some of whom would be asked to participate in the leading of worship. When I was the national Adviser on Health and Healing Ministries to the Methodist Church, I was invited to preach at one such service in Liverpool. A Christian doctor who was able and willing to speak at the service could be invited to be the special preacher.

In almost every section of this Worship Book there is suitable material for such a service. Look especially at THE SHALOM QUESTIONNAIRE, pages 157-159 and THE PREVENTIVE HEALTH CARE SERVICE on pages 160-162.

(I am indebted to the Revd. Bruce Thompson and to the Revd. David S. Owens for information about such Festivals)

167

IN QUIETNESS AND CONFIDENCE

Suggestions for a Healing Service including Relaxation, Meditation and Visualisation

(What is suggested here could, in whole or in part, be related to many different healing services. It will work best with a small congregation and whenever possible, seated in the round with a low table in the centre on which is placed a lighted candle and a cross and perhaps a floral arrangement. The framework only is provided here in three distinct sections. Some form of music will be necessary and quiet devotional hymns and/or choruses. These choices are left to those who decide to make use of this framework. There is plenty of material in other parts of this Worship Book which could be used in this context.)

RELAXATION

(Those present are asked to sit comfortably, holding nothing in their hands. Legs need to be unfolded and hands placed lightly on knees or upon arms of chairs if these are provided.)

First of all we begin with our breathing. We need to breathe deeply using the depths of our lungs. Fast shallow breathing can produce hyperventilation which, in the long run, can be harmful. So we breathe in harmony together, slowly and purposefully, filling the lungs and holding there for a moment or two before we exhale. *(Guide breathing for a short time, say to the count of six.)*

Now we begin a conscious programme of relaxation starting with our feet, ankles and toes. The pattern is to bring each part of our body, in turn, into tension. Then when we can feel the tension to give instructions to that part of us to let go. As we do so we aid circulation and we feel warmth and a sense of ease. This requires practice but the benefits will soon be felt. We are going to progress upwards thinking deliberately and acting deliberately about each part of our bodies:

Calf muscles, knees, thighs.

The trunk from the waist downwards
hips, stomach muscles.

From the waist upwards —
chest, shoulders, upper back.

Neck, head, jaws, eyes.

Return to observe your breathing... Enjoy the comfort... Feel the warmth... the tingling sensations... Be thankful.

Now we have relaxed your outer being, but the benefits will soon be lost if we forget about what is going on inside. So we now relax our inner being by first thinking about...

Our anger. What are we angry about? Anger can be destructive but it can also be constructive... There is righteous anger which often leads on to positive social action. Recognise your anger and deal with it positively.

Our sense of frustration and disappointment. Any bitterness. Acknowledge that it is a reality but it will not be allowed to cloud your life.

Wrong relationships. What can we do to put them right? Should we try?

Any sense of sin or failure. Express sorrow and regret and receive forgiveness.

(In accordance with your tradition give the assurance of forgiveness positively and strongly.)

So now... be at peace... your sins are forgiven... let go and let God.

+ + + + +

MEDITATION

(Choose a verse of scripture which lends itself to easy divisions and work slowly through it. Here is one example)

I am THE WAY, THE TRUTH and THE LIFE.

The Way

Call up a picture of Jesus who "set his face steadfastly to go towards Jerusalem" knowing what lay ahead. This was *his* way. What is your way? If ever there are two alternatives walk along each of them in company with Jesus. Along one there will be a greater sense of peace. This is *your way*.

Meditate around the concept of *his way* being linked to *your way*.

The Truth

Recall Pilate's question, "What is truth?" In Jesus himself there is truth. This is our clue to purposeful living. We don't have all the answers but we have committed ourselves to Jesus who will share himself with us. Therefore we shall be part of *the truth* ourselves.

Meditate around the concept of the truth that is Jesus being the focal point of your life.

The Life

Life in company with Jesus is much more than mere existence. It has meaning and purpose and he makes his life available to us. Think of the Eucharist, the Service of Holy Communion. We take his life into ourselves and it becomes ours.

Meditate around this idea of your coming to life because you share the life of Jesus.

+ + + + +

VISUALISATION

(This carries on naturally from what has gone before. You now choose a Bible story and you are going to use your imagination and see yourself as being part of the drama itself.)

Read in Luke 8:43-48, about the woman afflicted with severe haemorrhages for twelve years.

Now build a visual image of Jesus in your mind. Each person present will have a different one, perhaps taken from a Bible or a picture. The image doesn't matter but remember that his nature and his name are love.

See the crowd — you are part of it. There is a crush... a smell of sweating bodies...there is fear abroad... but also hope.

You have got near to Jesus and you see the woman stretch out her hand and momentarily grasp the edge of his garment. You hear the conversation following upon the woman realising that her deepest needs had been met. Her faith and trust had played a significant part.

Now its your turn. You push nearer. You find that you can actually lay hold of his hand. You have a need — bodily need — emotional need — spiritual need. You believe that he can make all the difference. Touch him. Feel him.

What may happen?

A deep awareness of forgiveness... an opening up of your personality... a release from an inner burden... a healing or the commencement of a healing process...

> Healing power of Jesus Christ,
> fall afresh on me,
> Healing power of Jesus Christ,
> fall afresh on me.
> Touch me, stir me, unfold me, love me.
> Healing power of Jesus Christ,
> fall afresh on me.

Give thanks to God who has met you in Jesus.

Go in peace: the Lord *is* with you.

PRESCRIPTION FOR HEALTH

An idea for a Service designed to contribute towards healthy personal and community living.

(This suggestion is for an informal service with wide participation. After a devotional opening the passage is read fairly slowly. The leader then points to the individual verses or phrases and suggests an initial time of reflecting upon them each in turn. Then anyone is asked to offer a thought of their own — either developing the Leader's interpretation or offering their own. At several points in the proceedings the Leader suggests a time of prayer in which the points arising from the discussion are offered to God. There should also be appropriate hymns and choruses held ready to introduce into the service when it seems right to do so.

The Bible passage is Colossians 3:12-17. It is printed here from the Good News Bible with key words in italic. The numbers inserted do not relate to the verses but link the phrases with the key ideas which then appear below.)

THE BIBLE PASSAGE

You are the people of God; he *loved you* (1) and chose you for his own. So then you must clothe yourselves with *compassion, kindness, humility, gentleness and patience* (2). Be *tolerant* (3) with one another and *forgive* (4) one another whenever any of you has a complaint against someone else. You must forgive just as the Lord has forgiven you. And to all these qualities add love, which *binds all things together in perfect unity* (5). The peace that Christ gives you is to *guide you in the decisions you make* (6): for it is to this peace Christ has called you together in one body. And *be thankful* (7). Christ's message in all its richness must live in your hearts. *Teach and instruct one another with all wisdom* (8) Sing psalms, hymns and sacred songs; *sing to God with thanksgiving in your hearts.*(9) Everything you do or say should *be done in the name of the Lord Jesus* (10), as you give thanks to him through God the Father.

(1) LOVED BY GOD

How important to realise the importance of this. We cannot stop God loving us. This gives us dignity, value, a sense of worth. There is surely only one response we can make to this love.

> Yet this central truth is sometimes difficult to realise. There are those who say they despise themselves. Why? How can we help them to become aware that God loves them?

(2) CARE FOR OTHERS

Perhaps this is the way — by helping others to be aware of divine love through our human love.

> This is often difficult. But Jean Vanier says that it is the broken ones who lead us to our own brokenness and thus to Jesus. What does he mean?

(3) ACCEPT OTHERS

I find it difficult to accept those who do not think like I do. I may appear to do so on the surface, but within myself I do not. And what about those who threaten us?

Do you tend to stick with those who think like you? Would a bit of honest, open anger be helpful? Do we gain anything by guarding our real feelings so carefully? Does fear of change underline our rigidity?

(4) FORGIVE

In another service in Section 5 (page 133) we have heard about the healing power of forgiveness. Real forgiveness does something for the one who forgives.

> Do you need to forgive yourself for finding it difficult to forgive others? Jesus forgave the paralysed man's sins before he was healed *(Luke 5:17-27)*. Does this synchronicity of events happen today?

(5) LOVE GIVES INWARD UNITY

If any part of us can facilitate inward unity it is the spiritual part. Even people who are not religious in any formal sense feel the need for the spiritual dimension. An intelligent woman whose daughter was dying put it this way, "I don't like the expression 'spiritual', it's too loaded for me, but for want of a better word I feel that the spiritual part of us is indestructible and emerges again in some form". *(Zorza V & A/A Way to Die)*

> How does the spiritual part of us bind us together? What helps you when you feel all mixed up inside? Does it help when someone says, "I love you"?

(6) ABLE TO MAKE DECISIONS

How difficult this sometimes is. Years ago I recall being given three words — Reflect — Evaluate — Decide. Sometimes those who are always making big decisions seem hard and unbending. Others seem to wrestle in anguish, totally unable to decide. The verse suggests that the peace given by Christ is the determining factor.

> How does this work out in everyday life? Should we not agonise when decisions are so hard to make? Perhaps those three words can be of help, providing they are set

within the Christ context. How do you feel about your own decision making processes?

(7) THANKFULNESS

A quality so often lacking. We take so many things for granted and totally forget to give thanks. Why not practise a bit more thankfulness in human relations? Then we may be more genuinely thankful in relation to God.

> Just dwell upon what Jesus has done:
> Loved us... Shown us the Father's face.
> Lived for us... Died for us... Rose for us.

> And be thankful.

(8) DISCOVERIES COME THROUGH SHARING

Sharing is costly. Sharing is demanding. Sharing releases vital energies between the sharers. Sharing requires trust. Sharing creates community. Sharing promotes growth.

> Who are the people with whom you feel you can share?
> Have you been let down?
> What happens to those who keep themselves to themselves?
> How can 'teaching and instruction' be combined with sharing?
> Who are the teachers you remember — and why?

(9) WORSHIP

Perhaps by this time we shall have some rich experiences to offer to God in worship. So we will do it rather than talk about it. However let us first look at the last point arising from the chapter.

(10) NAME THE NAME

The last thought is indeed a salutary one. It means that we
honour Jesus in every aspect of life — our marriages — our
relationships with our children — our work — our leisure —
and we give expression to that idea by naming the name.
Letting it be known where we stand.

> There are different ways of 'naming the name'. Some
> turn people off; others turn them on. What makes the
> difference?

And so we turn to worship which needs to include singing for
this is specifically mentioned in the passage. But sing with
integrity and praise with meaning for what you have discovered
from the Word and from each other.

Bless each other in The Peace and say a mutual grace together.

Section 7

SEVEN SETS
OF
QUOTATIONS, SENTENCES ETC.

SEVEN SETS OF QUOTATIONS, SENTENCES, ETC.

HEALTH

1. Health is a state of complete physical, mental and social wellbeing; it is not merely the absence of disease or infirmity, it is a fundamental human right.

> *(Alma Ata Declaration — World Health Organisation 1978)*

2. Health is a dynamic state of well-being of the individual and society, of physical, mental, economic, political and social well-being; of beings in harmony with each other, with the environment and with God.

> *(Christian Medical Commission of the World Council of Churches, 1982)*

3. Health is a complete and successful functioning of the human being, in harmonious relationship with every part, and with the relevant environment.

> *(Dr. Leslie Weatherhead in Psychology, Religion and Healing, 1951)*

4. Health is the ability to respond in a mature way to life as it is.

> *(Dr. Michael Wilson in The Hospital — A Place of Truth, 1971)*

5. What we are seeing is a new perception of health; not so much as absence of physical symptoms as enrichment of life through social interaction and a wide variety of meaningful forms of communication and relationship. This changes the focus of healthful considerations from biology to psychology and religion, from survival to meaning and purpose.

(Dr. Edgar Jackson in Understanding Health, 1989)

6. Health, in the Christian understanding, is a continuous and victorious encounter with the powers that deny the existence and goodness of God. It is a participation in an invasion of the realms of evil in which the final victory lies beyond death, but the power of that victory is known now in the life-giving Spirit.

(Tübingen Consultation, 1964)

7. True health is the strength to live, the strength to suffer, and the strength to die. Health is not a condition of my body; it is the power of my soul to cope with varying conditions of my body.

Jürgen Moltmann in The Power of the Powerless, 1983)

HEALING

1. Christian Healing is Jesus Christ meeting you at the point
of your need.

    (Bishop Morris Maddocks in a TV AM interview)

2. By his broken body,
      we, the body of humanity,
      are made whole,
      whoever we are and wherever we are,
      whatever our doubts or shame,
      our turmoil or anger.
      We are healed and can come together
      in the fulness of the Body of Christ.

    (Jean Vanier in The Broken Body, 1988)

3. When I work with a patient, I work with all four quadrants
of their being — the physical, emotional, intellectual and
spiritual. The only way to help them... is to offer them
unconditional love. Above all the person must rekindle hope in
life. Hope is the strongest medicine I use. Hope and Love.

    *(Dr. Hetty Rosenberg, a New Zealand Doctor in the URC
    Prayer Handbook, 1992)*

4. What may be needed most, at this time in our Christian
history, is a renewed recognition of the genuine tension that
exists between the grace that heals and the grace that enables
endurance. In that renewed recognition, there is some hope
that the balance will again be restored.

    (Lindsey P. Pherigo in The Great Physician, 1983)

5.   Healing is a miraculous phenomenon and one of mankind's greatest gifts. To me, the one continuous thread that wove together all the good healers I met was their capacity for unconditional love. I think therein lies the magic. It brings with it the gift of wings and the freedom to soar to a place where anything is possible. So much illness arises as a defence against life — a coping strategy. Gradually dismantling the defences means allowing the life force to flow in. Health is more than an absence of disease, it is an embracing of life.

(Allegra Taylor in I Fly Out With Bright Feathers, 1987)

6.   In practice, the whole area cries out for co-operation between all agencies working for healing, on the theological ground that God is the source of all healing, and on the practical ground that proper referrals and the establishing of real confidence between the agencies would be of immense benefit to patients.

(Frank Wright in The Pastoral Nature of Healing, 1985)

7.   Becoming whole does not mean being perfect, but being completed. It does not necessarily mean happiness but growth. It is often painful, but, fortunately, it is never boring. It is not getting out of life what we think we want, but is the development and purification of the soul.

(John A. Sanford in Healing and Wholeness, 1977)

PRAYER

1. We are not saying that a gathered community's prayers can always bring exactly what we think we want, but such prayers can help to bring healing and new understanding, no matter what the outcome of the particular crisis, and we have seen these prayers transform the outcome.

> *(T and S. Emswiler in Wholeness in Worship, 1980)*

2. To pray for someone is to try and see them as God sees them and to love them as he loves them. Not surprisingly, when that happens the relationship with them changes...
There is a way of loving in prayer which brings you into the depth of things... ...Finding each other in God is the heart of community life.

> *(Brother Bernard SF in Open to God, 1987)*

3. When we pray with people for healing we should pray for the healing of spirit, mind and body, for they are closely inter-related. Whatever affects one of these parts of our being has an influence of one kind or another on the other two... This approach means that we do not like praying only for the health of the body. I normally start to pray for spiritual, mental and emotional healing before I pray for the well-being of the body.

> *(Benedict Heron in Praying for Healing, 1989)*

4. Because the kingdom of God has not yet fully been revealed, we cannot say that every prayer for healing will be effective in curing every disease or in postponing death. Healing is one of the most striking manifestations of the

redemption of our bodies which salvation can bring; but it is an anticipation graciously and mysteriously vouchsafed to some, and, equally graciously and mysteriously, withheld from others. Complete wholeness of body, mind and spirit belongs to eternity; the prayer of faith acknowledges that.

(John Gunstone in The Lord is our Healer, 1987)

5. When we pray for people (sick or whole) we are loving them in Jesus.

(Author in Healing IS Wholeness, 1987)

6. In solitude we discover that being is more important than having, and that we are worth more than the result of our efforts. In solitude we discover that life is not a possession to be defended but a gift to be shared. It's there we recognise that the healing words we speak are not just our own, but are given to us; that the love we can express is part of a greater love; and that the new life we bring forth is not a property to cling to but a gift to be received.

(Henri Nouwen in Out of Solitude, 1974)

7. This is how to begin the day, not in your own effort but in the power of God. Awake to this fact and it will help you to arise — not only to get up, but to get over so many things that would pull you down. The way to overcome gravity — and so much triviality — is to arise in the Presence each morning. To know that we are the sons and daughters of God, that He is with us and that He gives us life eternal. He gives today a resurrection quality and helps us to *arise*.

(David Adam in The Cry of the Deer, 1987)

INTRODUCTORY SENTENCES

1. May the holy name of Jesus be our health today and always.

>   *(Morris Maddocks in A Healing House of Prayer, 1987)*

2. God says to each one of us: You are precious in my sight and honoured, and I love you.

>   *(Isaiah 43.4)*

3. Father God, we need you to love us... Jesus, we need you to save and heal us... Holy Spirit, we need you to bring home to our hearts the truth that we are loved and we can be both saved and healed.

>   *(HB)*

4. Lord Jesus, we stretch out our eager hands to touch you. We may only reach the hem of your robe but, like one of old, our touch is combined with trembling faith. May we hear you saying to us: "Your faith has saved you, go in peace".

>   *(HB and Luke 8:48)*

5. We come to God whose light illumines all creation, the Creator of all from the beginning. He was, he is, and for ever he shall be. He is in all and sees all.

>   *(Sventasvatara Upanishad in A Time for Salvation)*

6. God has broken into human history.
   God has raised Jesus from the dead.
   The whole human situation is changed.
   Righteousness is vindicated.
   Darkness is defeated.
   Hallelujah.

   (The author in Healing Experiences, 1985)

7. Come to share God's refreshing grace.
   Come to receive the assurance of forgiveness.
   Come to be restored and made whole.
   Come with a deep desire for things to happen in our midst.
   Then rest assured — they will.

   (HB)

SENTENCES FOR THE LAYING ON OF HANDS

1.   May the grace of our Lord Jesus Christ and the Love of God and the fellowship of the Holy Spirit meet all your needs and make you whole in body, mind and spirit.

2.   May the healing grace of our Lord Jesus Christ cast aside all the powers of darkness, bringing you an awareness of his gracious forgiveness. Rest in the power and strength which is available in Jesus, Trust him for "They who trust him wholly, find him wholly true".

3.   In quietness and confidence shall be your strength.
     In returning and resting shall you be saved.
     Jesus said: "I am come that you might have life and have it more abundantly".
     Ask and you will receive, seek and you will find, knock and the door will be opened.
     May God's gift of wholeness be yours in Christ Jesus.

4.   May the healing mercies of the Risen Lord, present with us now, fill your whole being, body, mind and spirit and heal you.

5.   In the name of God the Father,
     may new life quicken your whole body.
     In the name of Jesus Christ,
     may you be made whole in Him.
     In the name of the Holy Spirit,
     may you be given that peace which passes understanding.

6.   May the Lord Christ grant you healing and renewal, according to his will. Go in peace.

(5 and 6 by David Dale)

7.   God spoke to the Apostle Paul in his inner being and said: "My grace is sufficient for you and my strength is made perfect in your weakness". May that word be yours in this moment of time and through the laying on of our hands. Go forth with his sufficient grace and in his robust strength — and the Lord himself go with you.

HELPFUL WORDS AND WORKS OF JESUS
from Alan Dale's *New World*

1. It's a good thing to be healthy. But we may have to risk
the loss of an eye or a hand sometimes; God's way must always
come first.

2. Living in God's way sometimes takes all the courage you've
got. You'll be alright — if you never give in.

3. People everywhere were amazed at what Jesus said; when
he spoke you had to listen. Everybody was talking about him in
all the country towns and villages. He used to speak to them in
their meeting houses and make sick people better. He couldn't
go into any town without people crowding round him; he had
to stay out in the countryside and people used to come to him
from the villages roundabout.

4. Come here to me all you who are tired with hard work, I
will put new life into you. Let me give you a hand and show
you how to live. I'll go at your pace and see you through —
and I'll give you the secret of a quiet mind.

5. No healthy tree grows rotten fruit; no rotten tree grows
healthy fruit. You can tell every tree by its fruit: from a thorn-
bush you don't get figs; from a bramble bush you don't get
grapes.

6. When you help people, don't blow your own trumpet like
people who are only pretending to be good; they want people to
say "He's a good fellow". Very good, they get what they want.
When you help people, don't let your right hand know what
your left hand is doing.

7. My words will outlive the world itself *(Jesus)*.

SEVEN SIGNIFICANT WORDS OR PHRASES

1.   HOLINESS is God's gift to those who seek a closer
relationship with God through Jesus. It is not the slavish
obedience of a series of laws but it is the fruit of love. In
addition to a discipli e of prayer the way of holiness also
requires a daily commitment to discovering God in the everyday
experiences of life.

2.   ANGER can be destructive, but it is part of life. The
Psalms are full of anger against God but anger which is often
transformed into praise and thanksgiving. When anger arises,
as it inevitably does, it needs to be examined and an attempt
made to understand what lies behind it. Then the question has
to be asked — how can my anger be used constructively to
fulfil the purposes of love? Anger sometimes needs to be
expressed in order for the angry person to find release
(catharsis). Pastoral situations sometimes need a client to be
encouraged to be angry. God understands even when the anger
is directed against Him.

3.   DARK NIGHT OF THE SOUL — From time to time
those who aspire to wholeness and holiness will pass through
the experience described as 'the dark night of the soul'. It is a
time of doubt and of feeling abandoned by God. Yet, in the
darkness, the thirst for God survives and the truth comes home
that God is in the darkness with us. Thus these unhappy
experiences can lead on to times of illumination and renewal.

4.   HEALING THROUGH DEATH — Sometimes desperately
ill people need to let go of life in order to experience love's
consummation in death. Questions about life beyond the
experience we call death are many and the answers are few.
The Bible verses ending in "Nothing can separate us from the

love of God in Christ Jesus our Lord'' (Romans 8:38-39) are the best answer. God is love and the purposes of love can never be defeated. Herein lies our hope. In him (Jesus) we put our trust.

5.   LISTENING — The ability to listen in a committed way is a healing ministry in itself. Much has been written about it and there are many simple, basic training courses available. There is a technique involved and this can be taught but it is the person of the listener which is of primary importance. People who have been willing to discover uncomfortable truths about themselves often make good listeners. This means conquering the overwhelming desire to do people good. Those who are in the depths of despair have a right to groan and complain and even be bitter. A listener who accepts people as they are can have an effective listening ministry.

6.   CHARISMATIC RENEWAL — PENTECOSTALISM — In 1971 the Vatican was in touch with representatives of charismatic renewal movements and the classical Pentecostal movement. They agreed upon the following statement: ''The essence of Pentecostalism is the personal and direct awareness of the indwelling of the Holy Spirit, by which the risen and glorified Christ is revealed, and the believer is empowered to witness and worship with the abundance of life described in Acts and the Epistles. The Pentecostal experience is not a goal to be reached, nor a place to stand, but a door through which to go into a greater fulness of life in the Spirit. It is an event which becomes a way of life in which often, charismatic manifestations have a place. Characteristic of this way of life is a love of the word of God and a concern to live by the power of the Spirit''.

193

7.   THE EUCHARIST — "Every service is a healing service"
is an oft-quoted remark. True, although this does not rule out
the role of distinctive healing services. The Eucharist however,
presents the ideal pattern both for health and healing. The
important elements are Confession, Forgiveness, Thanksgiving,
Vision, Commitment to each other and to God. Think also of
making more of Touch — a gentle pressure of the hand when
the bread is given and eye-contact at the same time. There can
often be a quiet and unobtrusive 'laying on of hands' for those
known to be in special need.

APPENDIX 1

List of those who have made contributions to this Worship Book:

Dr. Patricia Batstone, B.A., M.Ed., 1, Higher Mill Lane, Cullompton, Devon. EX15 1AG.

Mrs. Julie Hulme, 8, Park Avenue, St. Ives, Huntingdon, Cambs. PE17 4JW.

The Revd. David Dale, B.A.,B.D., 23, Beech Drive, St. Ives, Huntingdon, Cambs. PE17 4UB.

The Rev. Dr. Eric J. Lott, 51, Clumber Rd., Leicester, LE5 4FH.

The Rev. Ivor W. Pearce, B.A., 46, South Rd., Northfield, Birmingham, B31 2QY.

Mr. Stanley W. Smith, 3, Loweswater Drive, Loughborough, Leics. LE11 3RR.

The Revd. Norman Wallwork, M.A., and Rev. Margaret Wallwork, The Birches, Crosthwaite Rd., Keswick, Cumbria, CA12 5PG.

The Revd. Veronica M.S. Faulks, B.A., The Manse, Newchurch Rd., Tadley, Basingstoke, Hants. RG26 6HN.

Permission has been obtained to reproduce items previously published, from the following:

The Iona Community, Glasgow, Scotland. (Wild Goose Publications) Authors: J. Bell and G. Maule.

APPENDIX 1 (Continued)

Stainer and Bell Ltd.,82, High Rd., East Finchley, London, N2 9PW. Author: The Revd. F. Pratt Green.

The Grail Community, 125, Waxwell Lane, Pinner, Middx. HA5 3ER.
Author: J. de Rooy.

Methodist Church Division of Ministries, 25, Marylebone Rd., London, NW1 5JR. *(Worship and Preaching)* Author: Dr. Patricia Batstone.

APPENDIX 2

Short quotations have been made from the following books or the books have been mentioned in this Worship Book. I have given all such details as are known to me and apologise in advance for any errors or omissions.

A HEALING HOUSE OF PRAYER by Morris Maddocks (Hodder & Stoughton, 1987)

LISTENING by Anne Long (Darton, Longman and Todd Daybreak, 1990)

AT EASE WITH STRESS by Wanda Nash (Darton, Longman and Todd, 1988)

PRAYER AND OUR BODIES by Flora Slosson Wueller (The Upper Room USA, 1987)

BY WAY OF THE HEART by Wilkie Au., SJ (Geoffrey Chapman, 1990)

PSYCHOLOGY, RELIGION AND HEALING by Dr. Leslie Weatherhead (Hodder and Stoughton, 1951)

THE HOSPITAL — A PLACE OF TRUTH by Dr. Michael Wilson (University of Birmingham)

UNDERSTANDING HEALTH by Dr. Edgar Jackson (SCM Press, 1989)

THE POWER OF THE POWERLESS by Jürgen Moltmann (SCM Press, 1983)

APPENDIX 2 (Continued)

THE BROKEN BODY by Jean Vanier (Darton, Longman and Todd, 1988)

URC PRAYER HANDBOOK, 1992

THE GREAT PHYSICIAN by Lindsey P. Pherigo (Abingdon Press, 1983)

I FLY OUT WITH BRIGHT FEATHERS by Allegra Taylor (Fontana-Collins, 1987)

THE PASTORAL NATURE OF HEALING by Frank Wright (SCM Press, 1985)

HEALING AND WHOLENESS by John A. Sanford, (Paulist Press, USA, 1987)

WHOLENESS IN WORSHIP by T and S. Emswiler (Harper & Row, USA, 1980)

OPEN TO GOD by Brother Bernard, SF (Fount Original, 1987)

PRAYING FOR HEALING by Benedict Heron (Darton, Longman and Todd, 1989)

THE LORD IS OUR HEALER by John Gunstone (Hodder & Stoughton, 1986)

OUT OF SOLITUDE by Henri Nouwen (Ave Maria Press, USA, 1974)

THE CRY OF THE DEER by David Adam (Triangle/SPCK, 1987)

APPENDIX 2 (Continued)

A TIME FOR SALVATION ANTHOLOGY Quotation by Sventasvatara Upanishad (Regina Press, USA.)

NEW WORLD by Alan Dale (OUP, 1967)

A RETREAT WITH THOMAS MERTON by Basil Pennington (Amity House, USA, 1988)

The following books by Howard Booth are also referred to in the text:

HEALING EXPERIENCES (Bible Reading Fellowship 1985). Now out of print.

HEALING THROUGH CARING (Arthur James Ltd., 1989)

STEPPING STONES TO CHRISTIAN MATURITY (Arthur James Ltd., 1991)

HEALING *IS* WHOLENESS (CCHH and Methodist DSR, 1987)

The poem by Louis Eveley in the Meditation on Psalm 139 I found in a Minister's study while on exchange in the USA. In the same meditation, the poem by A.J. Tessimond had been copied into one of my resource notebooks and so I am unaware of its source. Permission has been granted by the Oxford University Press to use three verses of Hymn No. 134 in *Hymns and Psalms* (MPH) by Rosamond Herklots. This is included in the Meditation entitled 'The Healing Power of Forgiveness'.